ALSO BY HESH KESTIN

Based on a True Story: Three Novellas

The Iron Will of Shoeshine Cats

THE

LIE

A NOVEL

HESH KESTIN

SCRIBNER

New York   London   Toronto   Sydney   New Delhi

SCRIBNER
A Division of Simon & Schuster, Inc.
1230 Avenue of the Americas
New York, NY 10020

First Scribner hardcover edition March 2014

SCRIBNER and design are registered trademarks of The Gale Group, Inc., used under license by Simon & Schuster, Inc., the publisher of this work.

For information about special discounts for bulk purchases, please contact Simon & Schuster Special Sales at 1-866-506-1949 or business@simonandschuster.com.

The Simon & Schuster Speakers Bureau can bring authors to your live event. For more information or to book an event, contact the Simon & Schuster Speakers Bureau at 1-866-248-3049 or visit our website at www.simonspeakers.com.

Jacket design by Eric White
Jacket photograph © Shane McCauley / Gallery Stock

Manufactured in the United States of America

1   3   5   7   9   10   8   6   4   2

Library of Congress Cataloging-in-Publication Data is available.

ISBN 978-1-4767-4009-6
ISBN 978-1-4767-4011-9 (ebook)

For
Chiara, Aidan, Shane, Lila, Noam,
Aviv, Maksim, Leora and Eliana.
In the hope they may live in peace.

There is among people no dividing line greater or more absolute than that between the happiness of some and the suffering of others. Affairs great and small divide people, yet none so sharply as the inequality of fate.

—*Holy Week,* by Jerzy Andrzejewski

Author's Note

No book is perfect, and no author.

The Lie is fiction, but it is fiction hung upon a framework of the real. Though I spent some twenty years reporting from the Middle East and have been to most of the places described in these pages, some locations may have changed since my last visit. In addition, memory does play its tricks. So if I have perpetrated the odd miscue, I beg the reader's indulgence and, should he or she wish to extend the favor, correction. These may be sent to me at heshkestin@gmail.com.

My last novel, *The Iron Will of Shoeshine Cats*, included one intended mistake. In a preface to that book I challenged readers to find it. In the three years it took for a careful reader to discover the error, other careful readers—to my shame and delight—discovered a dozen more.

Rather than learn my lesson, I have included in *The Lie* three intentional mistakes of fact—nothing egregious, nothing upon which the story hangs—but present nonetheless. I have no doubt that other errors will be brought to my attention, for which this author expects to be at once mortified, satisfied, and gratified.

Happy hunting!

HK

Prologue

Nearly forty-five years before our story begins, in a birthing room at Hillel Yaffe Hospital in Hadera, a city in central Israel, two children come into the world at almost precisely the same time.

The Arab mother has been silent through her long labor. Having borne seven children, she knows by now that screaming does not help.

The Jewish woman in the next bed is becoming a mother for the first time. The walls shake with her cries. She screams curses in one long stream until the child is out. The sweating doctor—there is no air-conditioning—tells her, "A boy—mazel tov!" He is smiling.

The midwife holding the other child shows less emotion. But she tries. "She is so pretty," she whispers. "A house full of girls brings happiness."

The Arab woman begins to weep almost soundlessly. In a moment the weeping swells into hysteria, her village Arabic peppered with the single word la! repeated over and over. It is Arabic for no.

Though neither doctor nor nurse speaks Arabic, each knows what the woman is saying and why she is saying it.

"Shall I give her the Abu-banat?" the nurse asks. It is an Arabic phrase well known in Middle Eastern obstetrics. Abu-banat means father of daughters, a curse for the father, a fearful burden of guilt for the mother.

"Ten cc's," the doctor says.

1

1

In the oak-paneled study of a comfortable Georgian home in the prosperous Westmount neighborhood of Montreal, Edward Al-Masri stops packing papers into his briefcase when he hears the doorbell. His rimless spectacles and academic tweeds are belied by a certain brooding intensity: His jaw is set, his eyes narrowed. Covered in a close thatch of premature gray—he is not yet forty-five—his large, handsome head is planted at an angle from shoulders that have never known physical work. His body seems a bit too small to hold it.

"Mr. Al-Masri?" Snowflakes the size of coins flood in with the Arabic. The taxi driver holds a wheeled suitcase high above the snow. It is the largest suitcase meeting the regulations of international airlines, but to judge by the way it swings from the driver's hand it is clearly empty.

"You're late."

"Praise Allah, a flat. Imagine. In this storm. First to take off the chains, then—"

"Late is late, *habibi*." The word—it simply means *my friend*—is uttered in a tone of near-feudal condescension. Al-Masri takes the suitcase from the driver. He looks at the snow coming down, the all-white street. In the taxi, a small flame momentarily lights up the dark rear seat, a lighter, not a match. He knows the man in the rear seat. He knows the man's gold lighter.

3

When he turns back to the driver, Al-Masri's reluctance is palpable, but the snow cannot be ignored: Arabs are taught hospitality from an early age. "Wait inside."

While the taxi driver stamps his boots on the grate and shakes off the snow that has already covered his shoulders and the stocking cap that warms his shaved head, Al-Masri rolls the suitcase into his study. He places it next to an identical one, a subtle tan plaid trimmed in blue piping, transfers his neatly folded clothes and a dozen books from one to the other, then disposes of his own empty suitcase in the rear of a closet. He locks the closet. Some things must remain secret, even from his wife. He wheels the new suitcase out of the room.

In the foyer, where the driver examines the book-lined walls with the awe of the barely literate, Genevieve Al-Masri holds their son. She brushes the fawn-colored hair from her face. "Kiss Daddy good-bye, honey," she says in the heavily metallic French of the Québécois. Many years before, Al-Masri published a book, adapted from his doctoral thesis, called *The Political Dimension of Language: Anti-Colonialism in Patterns of Inflected Speech*. It sold only a few copies, but was a beginning.

As Al-Masri embraces them, the toddler, suddenly aware that his father is leaving, begins to wail.

"Be careful, Edward," Genevieve tells her husband in English. "Those people . . ."

He winks, and follows the driver out the door.

The suitcase wheels are useless in the snow. The driver slips twice. Al-Masri does not reach out to steady him. He knows this much about himself: He loves his people in the abstract, less so when it comes to individuals. He knows this as well: He hates himself for it. This is why he will do what he is about to do.

2

The courtroom in Jerusalem is carpeted in a lush blue, apparently meant to echo the two blue bands and Star of David of the flag on the wall behind the three judges. The walls are paneled in a pale oak veneer. Oak forests covered much of northern Israel until the Ottoman Turks, who ruled the Middle East until 1914, built railroads that crisscrossed the Holy Land and fueled them with what was at hand. As a result, the number of old-growth oaks in modern-day Israel might be counted in the hundreds. Occasionally, solitary trees can be found like sentient monuments among the pine and fir of the reforested hills around Jerusalem. The oak panels in the courtroom are from Sweden.

Dahlia Barr, at forty-four a stark beauty whose face, long drained of softness, retains the glow of resilience, stands with the prosecutor before the judges. Her hair is the color of the oak veneer, shot with streaks of dramatic gray that pick up the color of her eyes. Her voice is clear, still young. "Your Honors, in any other situation, but a thirteen-year-old girl who is unable to communicate?"

The prosecutor breaks in. "Fourteen in two days."

"Thirteen, fourteen—a distinction without a difference," she says. "This is a child, perhaps not even capable of understanding the charges against her, a condition that will not be improved by further incarceration."

The presiding judge removes her glasses. "Prosecutor?"

"Your honors," he says with the sullen impatience of the put-upon. "This so-called child was carrying explosives, an undisputed fact. Does my learned colleague believe defendant received these explosives from an angel? Defendant received them from a human being. The state believes another week of careful and sensitive questioning will reveal—"

"Sensitive questioning? The child is both deaf and mute. We might as well have her on the rack. Does my respected colleague not have children?"

"My children do not carry bombs."

The judges confer in a whisper. "Forty-eight hours more," the presiding judge says.

Across the courtroom, a translator signs to the young girl. She immediately begins shaking her head. This sets off her family who, as one, shout imprecations at the judges, the court, the state.

Dahlia has seen this often. It is, she knows, a paradox: Palestinian Arabs believe cursing will improve the result, reflecting at once resentment against Israel and faith that the same Israel will not, as would any court in the entire Arab world, imprison them for it, even kill them. But she is a mother, too. She thinks, *Can any mother be blamed for losing her self-control in such a situation?*

The presiding judge bangs her gavel repeatedly.

It is minutes before Dahlia can speak. "After which defense respectfully requests defendant be remanded to an appropriate *juvenile* facility."

The presiding judge bangs her gavel once more. "So stipulated."

6

THE LIE

The prosecutor turns to Dahlia. "My children could have been on that bus."

Ignoring him, Dahlia approaches the sobbing girl as her large family gestures angrily behind the child. Unable to communicate with the girl, she places a hand on her shoulder. The family will have none of it. Now they are cursing *her*.

3

As the taxi plows sullenly through the Montreal snows, Fawaz Awad sits behind the driver puffing on a Gauloise in a gold cigarette holder. The left side of his heavy face is scarred, perhaps from burns, his thick glasses framed in gold with the left lens blacked out. In his mid-fifties, he is elegantly dressed, his left sleeve folded and pinned at the elbow. A cashmere overcoat is neatly arrayed on the seat between the two passengers.

"The Jews have one weakness," he says. "They will fight to the last child. They will clean up the blood and broken glass so that an hour from the worst attack, there is not a sign. They do business, conduct scientific research, write novels, make love." He sighs for effect. "But they hate when the world condemns them. Funny, no? We send thousands of rockets over their cities, and they laugh. But when the UN declares them to be criminals, they cry and tear their hair: 'Oy vey—nobody loves us!'" He laughs. "Praise Allah, this is not an Arab trait."

Al-Masri cracks the rear window against the veil of smoke. "Praise Allah," he says, not bothering to hide the cynicism. He has not seen the inside of a mosque in years.

4

In South Lebanon, Tawfeek Nur-al-Din stands at the edge of a high cliff overlooking the Israeli border. Still fit at forty, he is one of a rare group of Palestinian military commanders who has learned to emulate the example of the officer corps of his enemy: He does not lead from a desk; he leads by doing. Trained in Libya and Afghanistan, Commander Tawfeek carries with him the aura of personal martyrdom that is standard issue among Palestinian military leaders. Though he makes a point not to speak of this painful subject, it is said that his young wife and son were killed in an Israeli bombing raid over Gaza on the fiftieth anniversary of Al Naqbah, the Catastrophe, when the normally fractious Palestinians unite to commemorate their bitter loss in the struggle that Israel calls its War of Independence.

There was no Israeli bombing raid over Gaza on May 15, 1998. Commander Tawfeek's wife and two children are safely abroad. He does not know how the legend began. Nor does he care. A Palestinian military commander must have an aura. He has no tanks.

On the high cliff, twenty-one intensely trained black-garbed commandos face their leader, each strapped into an identical black hang glider. They have been training with this equipment for months.

9

Tawfeek raises his own glider wings, holds a wetted finger to the wind, winks theatrically, then breaks—with the wild improbability of a Bollywood film—into sweet Arabic song.

> *No wind today,*
> *A sign for tomorrow*
> *When our young martyrs will*
> *Fall upon the filthy Jews*
> *Like hawks upon rats,*
> *Like eagles upon snakes.*

His fighters join in heartily for the rousing chorus.

> *O purify the Muslim lands*
> *Of Jews and Christians and their bands*
> *Of rapists, murderers and thieves,*
> *Devils' dung who won't believe.*

Tawfeek holds up his right hand. "Praise God. Follow me now for one final practice flight. Radios off." With a flourish, he lights a cigarette from a pack marked Liban, then leaps, the others jumping after by threes. Seen from below, the black wings of their gliders all but eclipse the sun.

5

At Montreal International Airport, a young El Al security inspector questions Al-Masri while an assistant—like the inspector, an Israeli graduate student enrolled at a Quebec university—carefully examines his suitcase, which has already gone through an automated check for traces of explosive. This is the backup check, concerned as much with conversational nuance as with physical detection. Machines interrogate poorly.

The security inspector scrutinizes the two passports she has been given, then asks in English: "Who is Mohammed Al-Masri?" Her tone is even, friendly.

"That is I," Al-Masri says.

"And who is Edward Al-Masri?"

"The same."

"Two names, two passports, one person?"

"In Israel I am known as Mohammed. I use Edward professionally. I changed my name legally upon becoming a Canadian citizen."

She switches to Hebrew. "And what, professionally, does such a citizen do in Canada, Mr. Al-Masri?"

"I am a professor at McGill University. You may also have seen me on television. CBC, CNN. I am an author as well."

"You speak very good Hebrew."

"As both my passports indicate, I was born in Israel. Pardes

11

Hanna Agricultural High School, Haifa University. The complete sabra."

"You served in the Army, then?"

"Arabs are exempt from conscription."

Less friendly: "But not from volunteering. The purpose of your visit to Israel?"

"To see my family. And to do research for a book."

"A book about what?" She has switched back to English.

"The struggle for a just peace."

The security inspector looks to her colleague, who whispers something as she shakes her head: Nothing in the suitcase.

"That may take more than a book, professor. Have a pleasant flight."

As Al-Masri moves into the El Al waiting room, the security inspector picks up a phone.

6

At the taxi stand outside Jerusalem District Court, Dahlia opens the door of the first cab in line. From down the street, another Mercedes taxi pulls suddenly ahead of it. A muscular man in blue jeans and dark glasses jumps out of the front passenger seat. "Madam," he says. "You'll find this taxi is better."

As she stands holding the door of the first taxi, Dahlia's driver lets loose in primal Hebrew. "You see the queue, ass-wipe?" he shouts. "Find the other end of it. I've been sitting here for an hour!"

The newcomer flashes an ID. "We're a special taxi."

Dahlia gives him a withering look. "*Habibi*, I have a taxi."

"Ours gets you to Tel Aviv faster. We don't stop for red lights."

"Who says I'm going to Tel Aviv?"

"Zalman Arad."

This gives her pause. "If Zalman Arad wants to see me, he can make an appointment." She watches as the driver of the taxi that is clearly not a taxi gets out and looks impatiently at his watch. "Why does Zalman Arad wish to see me?"

"To tell you the truth, Ms. Barr, Zalman Arad doesn't con sult with me about such matters," the man with the ID tells her. "You've got two choices. Sit in the backseat or sit in the trunk. It's all the same to us."

7

Seated next to Al-Masri in business class, an older man in skull-cap, goatee, and vested suit whispers a request to the El Al flight attendant.

"You object to sitting with an Arab?" Al-Masri says. He is not whispering.

"Sir, I have Arab friends. Edward Al-Masri is not one of them."

8

In the rear of the speeding taxi, Dahlia answers the insistent cell phone in her purse. "What is it, Dudik?"

"I filed. This morning."

She looks out the window as the taxi winds down the highway past the orange-painted vehicles strewn like abandoned toys by the side of the road, the remnants of trucks destroyed by the Arab Legion as they sought to relieve a besieged Jerusalem in 1948. "Mazel tov," she says. "Assuming a fair settlement, I won't contest. Just let's keep it out of the papers."

"I moved some of my things this morning, after you left. I'll come by for the rest. Hopefully, you won't be there. I don't need tears."

"Dudik, what a prick you are. Tears would be the last thing. I stopped feeling anything for you years ago."

"In that we're equal."

"We have to tell the boys." She hears silence. "I said—"

"I told them."

"*You* told them? When?"

"I phoned Ari at his base last night. Uri I told this morning before school, the minute you left." He paused. "I was watching from the road."

"I'm the last to know?"

She snaps the phone closed, dropping it in her purse, staring

15

blankly out the Mercedes window as the hills level out abruptly to the green fields of a well-watered Israeli winter, groves of orange trees already heavy with fruit, the orderly barracks of chicken farms that always bring to her mind the images of certain camps in Poland and Germany that she considers the cultural baggage of the Israeli Jew. To a citizen of any other country this would be a shocking connection; to an Israeli it is merely appropriate. Lamp shade: skin. Railway cattle car: concentration camp. Tattoo: Auschwitz. When the first Holocaust survivors were brought here after the war, mean Israeli children called them *soap*. Dahlia's late father had taught her to say *cleansing bar* instead. He could not bear to say *soap*.

In a few minutes a road sign comes up for Ben Gurion Airport. They pass the exit. She reaches into her handbag for her phone.

9

Close to the Lebanese border, half-hidden in an apple orchard under camouflage netting, three Israel Defense Forces jeeps stand lined up next to a small tent, its flaps raised like wings. A twenty-year-old lieutenant is playing serious dominoes with his sergeant, a Bedouin tracker called Salim, who passes him a thick joint. The lieutenant in turn passes it to a grease-spattered corporal working under the closest of the jeeps.

"When you come to the Negev, I will show you a real tent," the Bedouin says. "Not made of canvas from a machine, but of pure black wool from goats, loomed by hand."

The lieutenant exhales. "If you've got more shit like this, I'll fucking move in." He checks his watch. "Yudka," he tells his driver under the jeep. "We're on the line in two hours."

Yudka is all of nineteen, a chubby boy with acne and only two goals in life: to drive for a general and to have a girlfriend. "It'll be ready, Ari."

The lieutenant pushes over the dominoes, sprawling back on the stony ground. "Wake me when it is."

Just then his cell phone rings. He reads the number flashing on the tiny screen. He lets it ring.

"Girlfriend?" the tracker asks.

"Worse. My mother." He pauses. "How's the Bedouin divorce rate?"

17

"Negligible," the tracker says. "Should I marry and tire of my wife, I can get three more. Not so my mare. There is none like her. Let me tell you, Ari. They say we are primitive. We are not primitive. We are practical."

Ari pulls the brim of his forage cap down over his eyes. "Jews smart," he says. "Arabs lucky." He is asleep.

"Or if the first wife gives me only daughters," the tracker says.

10

At the Kiryah military compound in the center of Tel Aviv, a bored sentry examines the taxi's occupants, then waves it through.

Once a pleasant neighborhood of two-story homes, the Kiryah is now headquarters of the Israel Defense Forces and certain of the nation's security services. Except for the strange fact that everyone on the cracked concrete pathways is in uniform, the Kiryah might be a red-roofed holiday village. Below ground, tunnels lead to three floors of bombproof reinforced concrete command bunkers.

The cab draws up before a building unmarked but for a stenciled number.

"Last stop," Dahlia's escort announces from the front passenger seat. "You know where to go?"

"I know where to go," she says.

Inside at a battered desk, an eighteen-year-old soldier, M-16 slung over the back of her chair, peers studiously into a compact mirror as she applies lipgloss. "Name?"

"Dahlia Barr."

The girl checks the computer in front of her. "The left-wing attorney? From the newspapers?"

"The human-rights attorney."

The girl points with her lipgloss to a staircase on the right, its worn marble steps once a luxurious architectural detail. Now the steps are chipped, cracked, stained.

On the third floor Dahlia passes open doors, each framing an officer on the phone or facing a computer. At the end of the corridor she pauses before a west-facing window. It looks out over the city to the wall of hotels lining the beach.

The voice that greets her is familiar, yet spectral somehow, the voice of a powerful ghost. "Have yourself a good look. They're building another hotel. Soon we won't see water at all."

Behind a tidy plywood desk in a small office sits a small, tidy man, skin olive against his shock of unruly snow-white hair. At seventy-five, he is still wiry, his intensity all but hidden beneath the perplexing calm that conceals an intimate knowledge of the strategic risks facing the State of Israel. He stands as Dahlia enters. His trim mustache is as white as his pressed open-collar shirt.

"I can remember when out these windows was nothing but blue," he says by way of greeting.

"I can remember when I was your student."

"The best law student I ever had. And the most charming."

"I'm not sure of the protocol. Do I kiss you or salute?"

He motions like a beloved uncle, but they embrace with strained formality. "You were always my favorite, Dahlia."

"Somehow I feel I let you down."

A red phone lights up on the plywood desk. He picks it up. "Tell the prime minister I'll call back." The prime minister could be voted out tomorrow; the security establishment is forever. He smiles. "Only in Israel could we elect such a clown. How could you let me down?"

"Politically."

"Because you defend those I would hang?"

"Something like that. Though as you know, hanging is now forbidden."

"Unfortunately," he says. "Dahlia, Dahlia. In a democracy,

even the worst scum must be defended in court. And you defend them so well."

"Why am I here, Zalman?"

"And the lads?"

"Ari is a lieutenant, paratroops. Uri enters the Army in September."

"The Jewish State in the hands of its infants. I saw them last at the young one's bar mitzvah. Such beautiful boys."

"Not to put too fine a point on it, but Zalman Arad never sits down to a meeting without already knowing everything about the person opposite. So why do you ask?"

"Dahlia, sometimes I think you are too much like me."

"Except we are on different sides of the political divide."

"Only within Israel does this seem to matter. The cousins see only filthy Jews." *Cousins* is the term Israeli Jews commonly use for Arabs, Jews and Muslims being descended from one father, Abraham. The irony is implicit.

"Why am I here?"

He pushes a paper across the desk, then a pen.

A glance tells her what it is, but not why. Another person would give in, if only to learn what signing it will reveal. "The Official Secrets Act? I can't sign this."

"You have Zalman Arad's word it will not affect your role as a defense attorney."

"And if Zalman Arad is hit by a bus?"

"Let's hope not. But I take your point." He moves the paper and pen back to his side of the plywood desk. "Dahlia, you may not be aware that we are in the midst of a massive reorganization of the security apparatus."

"There are rumors."

"The state faces an evolving threat."

"I deal every day with the state's evolving efforts to contain that threat."

"The cousins in Gaza are determined to wipe us out. In Lebanon the same. Iran will soon have nuclear weapons. Pakistan already. And now another front."

"What are you saying?"

"According to growing intelligence, we face terror from within."

Dahlia laughs derisively. "It's never happened. They are Arabs, but they are Israelis."

"They are twenty percent of the population, thirty percent among those of school age. In Algeria, five percent was enough to wear down the French. Terror is unpleasant, more so when it is homegrown." He pauses. "We have information our enemies are now attempting to incite our fine Arab citizens to violence. Never mind that Israeli Arabs are not exactly lining up to emigrate to Gaza or Ramallah—apparently, living in a democratic society under the rule of law is habit-forming. But there is always the disaffected youth. These can be influenced." He drums his fingers on the desktop. "I am not telling you a secret when I mention that we are currently negotiating with Washington for a massive arms deal. Certain persons wish to torpedo these negotiations. They wish to cause an uprising within Israel that will have a negative effect on public opinion in America. An internal intifada." Another pause. "I will not allow this to happen."

"We do have criminal courts. Your people picked me up outside one of them."

"Sometimes pragmatism must trump principle."

"Pragmatism must trump the rule of law? Is that what you're saying?"

Arad sighs. "Let us conjecture. Say we find a certain young Arab citizen is part of a group planning to attack a train, a bus, a school. We don't know where, but we know when. The courts by nature are . . . procedural. Motions, counter-motions, counter-

22

counter-motions. Let us say we have only twenty-four hours. Would you not agree we must consider extraordinary means?"

She lights a cigarette. "Do I understand you correctly?"

"I think you do."

"The State is now considering torture of its own citizens?"

"Extraordinary means. If it will save lives."

"Torture, Zalman?"

"How many Jewish children would you expend for a principle, Dahlia?"

"I don't deal in the hypothetical. As you taught me, it makes bad law."

"This is not about good or bad law. This is about survival."

"Where have I heard that before? Russia? Syria? China?"

He waves his hand. It parts the smoke. "In such places, these practices are utilized to preserve those in power. Here we would take such steps to preserve *lives*. Innocent lives. Many innocent lives."

"It never works. And I can't imagine why you are telling me this."

"Listen, then. As I speak, elite units are being transferred to the Police from the Army and the security services. We are bringing in key officers, specialists, the best. The state will not be threatened from within."

She laughs. "The Israel Police is unable even to patrol the roads."

"That is exactly why we are augmenting its abilities."

She rises. "With all due respect, Zalman . . ."

"I have not finished."

She sits. "So the Police will decide whom, when, and how . . . to torture? How does this concern me?"

"As a defender of civil rights, are you not concerned?"

"How does this *relate* to me?"

"Someone must make such decisions."

"Zalman, I can only pray for the man who must carry this burden."

"You may pray. But it will not be a man. Dear Dahlia, it will be you."

She stubs out her cigarette. "Zalman, you are mad."

"Because?"

"Because I have dedicated my entire life to the cause of human rights. You expect me to take part in a practice that is its anathema?"

"Who better, Dahlia? Soldiers, policemen, academics, politicians, bureaucrats? None of these has your résumé, your instincts, your will to do the right thing until the last possible moment. Whom would you trust with such decisions? Someone else—or yourself?"

She looks at her cigarette stubbed out in the glass saucer. She stops herself from lighting another. "I need time."

"My dear Dahlia," the old man says. "You have none."

11

Edward Al-Masri pulls the tan plaid blue-piped suitcase off the moving belt and follows the man who would not sit next to him through the passage marked NOTHING TO DECLARE. A tired-looking customs officer in thick glasses waves the Jewish passenger through. Al-Masri is stopped.

"Is it your duty to harass only Arab citizens, or merely your pleasure?" Al-Masri says.

The customs officer points to the next table, where a colleague spills out the contents of the luggage of a black-bearded Hasidic Jew. Most of it is toys, the same toys. "I have a lot of children," the Hasid is saying.

The first customs officer asks, "Is this your luggage, Mr. . . . ?" He checks the passport in his hand. "Al-Masri."

"Professor Al-Masri."

"Mazel tov. Is this your luggage?"

"Are you accusing me of stealing someone else's bag?"

"Is it yours or someone else's?"

"Go to hell."

"Sweetie, my shift ends in ten minutes. Let's not make this more difficult than it has to be. Yours?"

"Very well, then. Mine."

"Purpose of visit?"

"This I was already asked at immigration."

25

"Humor me, Mr. Al-Masri."

"*Professor* Al-Masri."

"Pleased to make your acquaintance. Professor, doctor, mister, whatever. Believe me, this does not have to take long. A few questions, and you are on your way. Purpose of visit?"

"To see family."

"Where?" The customs officer opens the suitcase.

"Baka al-Gharbiya."

"Ah, Baka. I grew up next door. In Afula. Does Abu Adel still roast coffee there? I smell it in my dreams." The officer feels something in the suitcase lining.

"I haven't been back in five years. I now make my home in Canada, where Arabs are not punished for being Arabs."

The customs officer slits open the lining with a razor. "I didn't know that, professor. Tell me, are these Canadian? They look like euros to me." He begins to stack the banknotes on the counter. Seemingly out of nowhere, a couple of police constables appear and stand on either side of Al-Masri.

Rather than being startled, Al-Masri looks amused. "You people had police already in place? Do you have X-ray eyes?"

"Better," the customs inspector says, admiring the carefully stacked banknotes. "Our college girls in Montreal can feel a lump in a suitcase lining the size of a shirt button."

"Yet they let me board the plane? It could have been a bomb."

"All hand baggage is chemically scanned."

"Still, a passenger with contraband?"

The customs inspector removes his thick glasses to stare directly into Al-Masri's eyes. "Israel has no power of arrest in Canada, professor." He replaces his glasses and turns to the two constables. "These smuggled funds will remain with the Customs Service until we are otherwise advised." He turns to the constables. "Gentlemen, Mr. Al-Masri—excuse me, Professor Al-Masri—is all yours."

12

She knows Dudik is already at Moshiko's. Dahlia had wished to get there first, but the early evening traffic in Tel Aviv has been compromised further by a burning bus on Allenby Street, which the security people have closed off two blocks ahead of her and a block behind. Her taxi driver, a real taxi driver this time and remarkably relaxed for the breed—one A. Einstein, according to his name plate—returns from a closer look to report the bus was not bombed.

"Who would guess that it is not terrorist?" he says in a Russian accent. "Some gangster blows up the car of another gangster, and the car is next to the bus, which catches fire."

"Makes for a change," Dahlia says from the backseat.

Normally, she reads briefs while traveling. Now all she can think of is the strange prospect of seeing Dudik at Moshiko's, having willed herself to do so. Another woman might have lapsed into bitter nostalgia, remembering the two of them as they had been, young attorneys, Dudik in the pressed uniform of an officer in the Judge Advocate General's Office, she fresh from law school and finishing her apprenticeship, about to go out on her own. It was at Moshiko's he proposed. In the garden. No doubt he would be there now, peering down at his expensive watch, one of his many expensive watches. In the garden, for sure. It was where they had always sat, once in a light rain, laughing.

But Dahlia is not another woman. She remains focused on the need to avoid confrontation over the divorce, the one thing, aside from the boys, that ties them together, the only thing, really, the divorce, that has survived—

"There is a God," Einstein interrupts, starting his engine. The cars ahead begin to move.

If it had been a terrorist bombing, they would be there for an hour while the special squads of Orthodox Jews in their beards and fringes who volunteer for this gruesome work carefully comb the area for bits of brain, an ear, the odd finger, lest these pieces go unburied.

They pass the burned-out bus and the remains of a silver Volvo that seems to have melted into it, then turn right onto Ben Yehuda. The street has not changed much from the days of their youth. Apartments above shops, mostly small. Even the supermarkets here are small. Everywhere else, they are new and huge, American-style, with a dozen checkout counters. As they pass the Super-Sol off Gordon, she can see the same two checkout counters she had known when she and Dudik were just starting out and living a block away. The cab pulls in right behind Dudik's red sedan, the biggest one BMW makes.

It is the same Moshiko's, three tables on the sidewalk looking a bit forlorn on this cool evening, inside a ceiling fan turning slowly for no good reason other than it always did. She can already smell the rich, dark scent of grilling meat.

But it is not the same Moshiko who comes out from behind the refrigerated case full of kabobs, lamb and chicken, and *merguez*, the peppery sausage Dudik used to order with clockwork regularity until his stomach could no longer handle it. This Moshiko who embraces her could be Moshiko's own father, the same sharp-featured walnut-colored Yemenite face, the same knitted skullcap, the same scent. Eau de Moshiko, she used to call it. Equal parts slow-burning charcoal, some bizarre lemony cologne, stale sweat.

"Such a long time," Moshiko tells her when finally he lets her loose.

"Too long. I've been so busy with work."

"Funny," he says. "Dudik said precisely the same. He's in the back."

It is early. They are the only customers. She threads her way between the tables and out past the tiny kitchen, where an Arab cuts onions, and into the garden, such as it is: the unadorned back of a stuccoed apartment building forming a rear wall, a cactus too big for its pot, the same willow tree, in the far corner mint spreading over the big cement floor tiles that, twenty years earlier, had not been terribly straight. Now they are jumbled, nearly upended. She thinks, *Like everything else in my life.*

At fifty, Dudik Barr is graying but thick and confident in the way of self-made men. A former major in the IDF, he had spent a total of eight years in uniform when he retired as a military judge to take up private practice representing Israeli high-tech companies wishing to go public on Wall Street. Early on, he decided to forgo hourly fees and instead be paid in stock. As a result, he is now a director of seven companies, three in Tel Aviv and four in California.

When she enters the garden, Dudik stands.

That is one thing about my husband, she thinks. *He has always been an unerringly polite son of a bitch.* "A bus was burning on Allenby—"

"It was on the news. I heard it in the car." He sits when she does. "I took the liberty."

Before her is a shot glass of arak, the anise-flavored alcohol of the Mediterranean that, under so many names—raki, ouzo, pastis, sambuca, ojen, kasra—is common to its disparate cultures. Dudik used to laugh at her for preferring a man's drink.

"A hairy man's drink," he liked to say. These days he could not say it. Arak is now a popular drink among twenty-somethings in Tel Aviv. Dudik's own taste runs to single malt, the more expensive the better. There is a bottle of it on the table.

She pours the shot into a glass full of ice and tops it with an inch of water.

"Cheers," Dudik says. He never uses the Hebrew toast.

"*L'chaim.*"

"I ordered appetizers. I hope you're hungry."

"I can eat," she says. "That's why I'm so fat."

"You're not fat."

"In the twenty years of our marriage, I gained a pound a year."

"I gained two. So it's good we're divorcing. We'll be thinner."

"I told you on the phone, I'm not here to talk about the divorce."

He refills his glass from the bottle. INCHGOWER, the label reads, 14 YEARS OLD.

She guesses he brought it. Moshiko wouldn't know a single malt if it made a pass at him in a bar. She smiles at her own unspoken joke. "You always were such a snob."

"I've an appointment at eight, Dahlia." He sips from his Scotch. "Just to get this out of the way, you were right: I should have told you first. Not the boys."

She smiles. "Just to get this out of the way, that's not why I'm here."

"You're ill?"

"Do I look ill?"

For a moment his face darkens, its broad planes taking on a deep shadow all its own. "The boys?"

"Our young men? No, they're fine. I spoke with Ari earlier."

"It's quiet in the north," he says. It is as much an aspiration as a statement of fact. In the Middle East, statements of fact can be quickly undone.

"Thank God for quiet in the north."

"Am I to keep guessing?"

"I need your advice."

"My advice?" He lights a cigarette. "You don't want me in your life, but you want my advice."

"Exactly."

"I'm listening."

She had rehearsed some of this in her mind, starting with: "Dudik, I don't like you, but you're the smartest man I know." She does not bother with the introduction. She knows that in a similar case he would come to her. This is not a matter of the heart. It is a matter of the head. She goes through it for him, summarizing as though it were a legal brief.

"Head torturer of the State of Israel?" he says.

"Special Adviser for Extraordinary Measures to the Chief Commissioner of Police."

His lips purse for a moment, then straighten as his mind shifts into gear. "So what do you want to know?"

"Don't be obtuse."

"Obtuse? It's your decision."

"That much I know."

He sips from the Scotch. "Zalman Arad is using you to cover his ass. It's not personal, it's political. Zalman wants you because of who and what you are. If Dahlia Barr approves of— what are we calling it?—extraordinary measures, no one can say they are not critically necessary. What made you a pain now makes you an asset."

Moshiko brings a tray of appetizers. "Just like old times," he says. "You want to order?"

"This ought to hold us," she says.

When Moshiko goes away, Dudik completes his thought. *Human Rights Attorney Moves to Police.* It's a compelling headline."

"They intend to crack down on Israeli Arabs."

"I shouldn't think it's as general as that," he says with casual authority. "Something is happening, something specific. Something big."

"Big enough to trash the rule of law?"

"Big enough to have a prominent human-rights attorney do it for them."

"I won't."

He laughs. "Dahlia, we're discussing Zalman Arad. He doesn't look three steps ahead. He looks at the endgame. In some case where it will be necessary, some speculative, imaginary, even improbable case in which an Israeli citizen—not some crazed Palestinian from the territories but an Israeli citizen—must be, let us say, coerced using any means available in order to save lives . . ."

She picks up a stuffed grape leaf, then puts it down. "Zalman's words exactly." She pauses. "Would you do it?"

"I wasn't offered the job."

"And if you had been?"

"Never happen. But in terms of effectiveness . . ."

"I *could* make a difference. As things stand, this kind of decision, it's made by whoever happens to be in command. No checks, no balances. No rules."

"You *could* make a difference," he says. "Are you making a difference now?"

"Not much more than any other attorney." It is difficult for her to admit. Especially to Dudik. *Your powers are limited,* he used to say about her work. *Your intellect is wasted.*

"There's your answer. The government gets political coverage if and when extraordinary means must be used. You get to make a difference."

She tears off a piece of warm pita, dips it into the small dish of hummus, and brings it to her lips. "I get to make a difference, you get to make money." At once she regrets this. It is old news. And Dudik has been trying.

"Suddenly, the old Dahlia is back," he says. "You come to me for advice and then you turn on me. Look, I really do care."

"If you really cared, you wouldn't be breaking up a family."

"I'd love to know what this is about. I thought we were having a conversation about your career." He rises. "As I said, I have an appointment."

"You'd love to know what this is about?" she says, looking up at him. "It's about greed. Anger. Unwillingness to compromise. Ego. Bitterness." She pauses. "Pain."

"Pain." He allows a reluctant smile. "Agreed." In a moment he is gone.

13

From the rear of the unmarked police car climbing to Jerusalem, Edward Al-Masri peers out at the green winter landscape of central Israel, so much the opposite of Canada's. Here, winter is the only time it rains. How odd, he thinks, that in Canada winter is the barren season in which nothing grows, and in summer everything is in flower. Here, in summer the hot dry winds denude the fields. *Backwards, everything is backwards,* he thinks. His hands are tied behind him, his shoes removed so that in the unlikely event of an escape he will not be able to go far. Of course, the last thing on his mind is escape. Here in the backwards land of his birth, his usefulness will come only in captivity. In Canada, in America, in Europe, all his freedom has been meaningless, a talking head on television. Now that he is silenced, his voice will be heard. He will make a difference at last.

14

That evening in Caesarea, the beachfront village that is home to wealthy Israelis and well-heeled part-time Zionists who visit from time to time, Dahlia steps from her car to the open front door of a beautiful stucco home. Through the open French doors at the rear of the house she can see her seventeen-year-old son doing laps in the pool as, to the west, the sun has all but descended below the dunes lining the Mediterranean. She drops her bag on the foyer table.

At her approach, Uri climbs out, towels off. "Dad moved out."

"I heard."

He joins her on a chaise. "Mom . . ."

"Sweetie?"

"I'm glad it happened."

"My child . . ."

"I know it's been hard for you. Dad wasn't nice."

"I wasn't so nice to him."

"He has someone else. He told me."

"That was thoughtful of him."

"I told him to go fuck himself."

"Uri, he's entitled to live his own life."

"Not at our expense."

"Even at our expense, my sweet. Believe me, sometimes we must make decisions that cause pain."

35

"He could have been nicer to you."

"Your father and I, we weren't really cut out for nice. It happens."

"It's not supposed to."

"We're not supposed to be always in a state of war with our neighbors. House fires are not supposed to happen. Sickness. Your father did the right thing."

"Walking out? How is that right?"

"He should have done it earlier. I should have."

"Why didn't you?"

She looks away. "The pool needs cleaning. Promise me you'll clean the pool."

"Mom . . ."

Dahlia pauses. "All kinds of reasons, some better than others. You were the good reasons. You and Ari. The rest was just . . ."

"I know you have someone, too."

For a moment she is stunned, then oddly relieved. She laughs. It comes in a burst, a snort. "And I thought I was being so discreet. I know I was away a lot. I suppose the phone, the sudden hang-ups . . ."

Uri shakes his head. "Starting when I was in tenth grade, we knew. Ari and me, we knew."

"I tried not to—"

Uri shakes his head. "Starting in tenth grade. You began to look better. Healthier, almost. You smiled more."

"Oh, my little Uri." She is fighting tears.

"Plus, you were so much less bitchy. It was like you had a life."

15

The next day at a sidewalk table outside a café opposite Jerusalem's Mahane Yehuda Market, Floyd Hooper, thirty-five, television-handsome in a black CNN T-shirt, sunglasses well back on his head, lays down his *Jerusalem Post* as Dahlia sits. Behind them the market is alive with shoppers, the shouts of vendors boasting of the magnificence of their eggplants, the freshness of their tomatoes, the fragrant integrity of their olive oil. Through the smoke from his cigar he blows her a discreet kiss. Not for the first time does she wonder how it is that her husband and her lover both smoke cigars.

She looks around. "Shouldn't we be inside?"

"You are *so* late."

"In this part of the world the clocks have rubber hands. Perhaps inside would be better, no?"

"Who's going to see us? Besides, I'm a journalist, and you're my source."

"Of pleasure, I hope."

"You can't imagine. Now, tell me what's so important to get me out of bed this early in the morning."

"It's noon."

"Five A.M. in Atlanta. I ordered."

"When we break up, I'll never think of you without having to pass gas."

"But you love eggs with fava beans." He does a poor imitation of a character in a movie. "I ate his chopped liver with some falafel and a nice Manischewitz."

"Fool."

"For love."

"You are such a dummy. F-U-L. Meaning fava beans. It's not so terribly hard, is it?"

"Getting harder by the minute."

"Why do men think something like that is amusing?"

"Don't you just love me for it?"

"I do love you for it. The *ful* and the smelly cigar and never seeing you when I need to, that's just frosting on the cookie."

"Icing on the cake."

"That after four years here, someone with only five words of Hebrew—*hello, thanks, left, right,* and *blow job*—that such a person is correcting my English . . ."

"Such a person wants to know why you had to see me. It's not one of our days."

"I'm giving up my practice."

He stops relighting his cigar. "You're giving up your practice?"

"And getting a divorce."

He puts down the cigar.

"Kitten got your tongue?"

He laughs. "Cat."

"You are so cute when you're speechless, I could eat you up."

"Be happy to give you the chance," he says. "I've got the rest of the day off."

"Aren't there any Israeli atrocities you can blow out of all proportion?"

"It's a slow day for atrocities. Let me guess. You're getting a big fat settlement, so you've decided to stop defending the innocent. Anyone else, yes. You . . ."

THE LIE

"Even the noble grow weary."

"Why don't I believe you?"

"Because you're a liar by profession. All journalists are. So you can't believe everyone else isn't. It's called projection."

"God, I want to fuck you."

"I've an appointment at the Knesset. I'll be at your place by three."

He reaches across the table for her hand and squeezes it. "If you're as much as five minutes late, I swear I'll start without you."

As the waiter approaches, she withdraws her hand. "I'll never forgive my mother."

"For being a monster?"

"For not suggesting younger men."

16

The home of Israel's parliament, the Knesset, sits on a high hill with commanding views of a Jerusalem united under Jewish rule in 1967, but the view most often seen by its 120 members is as fragmented and cliquish as that in any high school cafeteria. Not only do members of its dozens of political parties rarely deign to dine together, but often their religious views mitigate against it.

Just as the design for the concrete and stone Knesset building became a cause for sociopolitical wrangling—its original exterior columns were transmogrified into bizarrely notched rectangles in order to avoid any reference to the classical architecture of Greece and Rome, the two cultures that all but destroyed the Jewish people—even its dining room became an issue: Eventually the facility was divided into two cafeterias, one for milk products and one for meat, because under Jewish law, foods containing either may not be mixed. Rabbinic supervision is so rigorous that several years earlier, when an Orthodox member of Knesset found a well-cooked cockroach in his meat loaf, the cafeteria was closed for a week until the entire meat kitchen could be cleansed: pots, pans, dishes, silverware, and everything else that might come into contact with food. The problem was not sanitary but dietary: Though Jewish law permits the eating of some insects—grasshoppers, for example—cockroaches are as unkosher as pork.

This culinary issue was apparently resolved, because as Dahlia crosses the meat cafeteria she sees that the room is again full of Orthodox Jews chatting noisily over their chicken soup or turkey schnitzel, none of them looking up as she passes, lest they display an impure interest in the female form. But as Dahlia moves through the more liberal tables a number of parliamentarians (and the newspaper columnists who fatten off of flattering them) greet her with a wave or a smile. At the far end, where the right-wingers congregate, her entrance is noted with clenched stares. *Once the news is out,* she thinks, *these will be the ones making noise: Why has a liberal been given keys to the torture chamber?*

Considering that this is the meat cafeteria, the two fiftyish men at the table where she stops are appropriately beefy. They abruptly cease conversing.

In the dark blue winter uniform of the Israel Police sits Chief Comm. Chaim Zeltzer, his massive shaved head glistening with sweat; opposite, in a brown suit, colorful shirt and clashing tie, is Daoud Idris, an Arab member of Knesset whose Hebrew is better than that of the Jew across from him, though it does carry a mild Arabic accent, the odd *p* sounding too much like *b*. Idris is known to delight in punctiliously correcting the Hebrew of Knesset members who did not have the good fortune to grow up speaking Hebrew. Neither man rises.

"Advocate Barr," Zeltzer says. "You're early."

"I'll be happy to wait."

"Not at all, dear lady," Idris says with oily courtesy. "We have completed our discussions." He looks her over. "So this is the famous Dahlia Barr. From the newspapers, I envisioned a larger woman, mannish in figure. Not such a . . . one." Her look does not encourage him. "Nevertheless, as a member of Knesset, I commend you for your record on behalf of the human rights of the Palestinian people. If ever I can help you in these virtuous

41

endeavors . . ." As if conferring a medal, he rises to present his card. "Chief commissioner, distinguished advocate."

Zeltzer makes a point of watching him walk off. "Pompous piece of shit. We let them into the Knesset and they act like they own it. So, Advocate Barr . . ."

"I'm pleased to meet you, too, commissioner."

"Chief commissioner. But please, call me Chaim."

"Dahlia, then."

"So we finally meet, though in truth, we have been close enough on many occasions. Your clients are my bastards."

"Were."

"So I am given to understand." Ignoring the empty cup in front of Dahlia, he pours himself coffee from the carafe between them. "Just so we are clear, I expect your full cooperation."

"We're on the same team."

"You are on my team. You will report directly to me."

"With pleasure. Except with regard to certain extraordinary matters. In these, my report is to the adviser to the prime minister for security affairs."

"Despite his saddling me with"—he pauses in search of the least offensive noun—"an outsider, Zalman Arad does not command the Israel Police."

"He commands me."

"This is not a good start, Dahlia."

"Chaim . . ."

"Yes, Advocate Barr?"

"With all due respect, sir, my brief is clear," Dahlia says. "Put another way, when you fuck with me, you are fucking with Zalman Arad."

He shakes his head. "I am not afraid of Zalman Arad. Do you think I am afraid?"

"We're all in his notebook."

"I have nothing to hide."

"I'm sure you don't, commissioner."

"*Chief* commissioner. You will report for duty tomorrow morning, seven forty-five. Sharp."

"As agreed with Zalman. We also agreed that I will take whatever time is necessary to arrange new counsel for my clients."

"Advocate Barr, I am not sure I prefer you outside the tent pissing in, or inside pissing out. Per agreement, your rank will be chief superintendent. You will be issued a pistol and a range specialist assigned. Be proficient by six P.M. Have you shot before?"

"I instructed in handguns in the Army."

Zeltzer does not look pleased. "The Army is less demanding. A car and driver will be assigned."

Dahlia watches him adjust his cap, walk away.

17

Through floor-to-ceiling penthouse windows the Old City below is postcard-golden. Dahlia smokes, she and Floyd post-coitally propped against a zebra-skin headboard. An ashtray sits on his abdomen.

"I hate it when you're silent," he says.

"You don't. You love everything about me. Admit it."

"You're such a bitch, Dahlia."

"A bitch is what you need."

"So you say."

"Admit it. Admit you love me. Admit you love me because I'm a bitch."

"I love everything about you. Bitch."

"Admit you've never had a woman like me."

"I never have."

"And that you'll never find better."

"Probably." He laughs. "I'm not looking."

"Me neither. We're the perfect fitting."

"Fit. Why are you giving up your work?"

"I'm not."

"You said you were."

"I said I was closing my practice."

He lays his hand on her breast, leaving it there like a lid. "Okay, it's official. I'm confused."

"How is that different from being a journalist?" She stubs out her cigarette. "I've accepted a position with the government."

"Bitch in chief?"

"I'm to work with the police as a kind of internal consultant."

"The police? You?"

"To protect the rights of criminal suspects."

"The police are interested in protecting the rights of criminals?"

"Suspects. The prime minister is moving to upgrade the department."

"Why?"

"Why is the prime minister upgrading the department, or why am I taking the job?"

"Both."

"Because it's been neglected. All the attention has gone to the Army and the security services. In this particular job, I *can* make a difference." She pauses. "Something I've failed to do in private practice. I'm sick of arguing against policy. Now I can help make it."

"Attention means what—funds?"

"You'll have to ask someone else."

"What am I not being told?"

"That I have to go."

"You always have to go. Sometimes I think you're with me only for the sex."

"And what's wrong with that?"

"You always have to go, that's what's wrong with it. It'd be nice to spend some time . . . vertical."

"I have something you don't." She switches to Hebrew. *"Mishpacha."*

"Those flaky cheese things?"

"The flaky cheese things are *bourekas.* Floyd, my darling, you've been here four years. *Mishpacha*: family."

"Americans can't do foreign words. *Bonjour, adios, shalom.*

That's about it. Pizza, lo mein. Could be a few more. Tiny brain, that's all."

She reaches under the covers, causing him to jump. "Lucky for me that's all that's tiny about you."

18

In the moonless sky over south Lebanon, vague shapes appear as minor disturbances in the darkness led by a tiny light as indistinct as a distant star. It is the smoldering end of a Liban cigarette clenched in the teeth of Tawfeek Nur-al-Din, flying ahead of his troops, their faces blacked out, their hang gliders eerily silent. Three hundred feet below, the border is unmistakable: dark on the Lebanese side, lit settlements on the Israeli.

19

Dahlia's headlights illuminate flowering orange trees while overhead sprinklers surround her with a steady, rhythmic *pshh . . . pshh . . . pshh* before hitting the car with a sound like slapped flesh. At the end of the dirt road is a small farmhouse. Even in the restricted glow of her headlights it is clearly neglected, its paint flaking, the stucco on its walls showing bald patches that reveal the concrete below. A dog runs out barking, then wags its tail in recognition.

She leaves the car without locking it and as she steps into the night air breathes in the fragrance of orange blossoms, heavy with perfume and promise. And memory. She stands for a moment before the door. It is ajar. She walks in.

Two older women sit in the small book-lined living room watching the television news. A round-faced politician is being interviewed. Dahlia's mother looks up. Erika is seventy, sharp-featured and austere. The other woman, whom Dahlia has always called Auntie Zeinab, the same age but softly maternal in Arab dress, rises to embrace her. Even before the death of Zeinab's husband, when Dahlia was four, the Arab woman was close to Dahlia's mother for no apparent reason. Six years later, when Dahlia's father died, the friendship deepened, a puzzle to Zeinab's neighbors in the Arab village down the road in Wadi Ara, and a conundrum to Dahlia as well. The two widows

could not have been more different. Even as a child Dahlia suspected that something other than an interest in far-left politics
united them, but she did not care. This way she could see Auntie Zeinab several times a week.

"Niece of my heart, when I don't see you I weep."

Dahlia is suddenly awash in the musty scent of her aunt's
clothes, her skin. She kisses her, then turns to her mother.
"Good evening, Erika."

"How good can it be? To live in such a time? Once we were
heroes."

"My darling niece, you look so tired," Zeinab says. "Let me
prepare mint tea."

"You always spoil her," her mother says.

"I am her second mother. I was present at her birth."

"As I was present at your son's. But you do not see me baking
him cakes, making him mint tea."

Zeinab is already in the kitchen. "You cannot," she shouts.
"He resides in Canada."

"My mother would not look after your son were he right here."

Zeinab steps back into the living room. "My dear niece, he
soon will be," she says in the careful and slightly formal Hebrew
of those whose native tongue is the sibilant provincial Arabic of
the villages. "Even at this moment he flies. He comes to write
another book."

Erika lights a cigarette, the cheapest local unfiltered brand,
packed in plain paper, no cellophane. The harsh tobacco is so
dry it flares. "All his books will not bring justice. We live under
fascism."

"Erika, I came to tell you I—"

"What, that you continue to support the government by pretending to defend its victims in its kangaroo courts? That your
obscene husband continues to make millions while Palestinian
children starve?"

"No Palestinians starve, Erika. You know that. What I've come to tell you is that you will no longer have to suffer his obscenity."

Zeinab enters with a tray.

"Dudik and I are divorcing."

"My dear niece! How awful for you."

"It's mutual, auntie."

"From birth I have loved you as my own daughter, praying daily for your happiness. Now this. And the children. How difficult for them."

"Her children are already ruined," Erika says. "One an officer in an army without morality, the other soon to join him. Your father, Dahlia, would shudder at what has become of his daughter, his grandsons, his land."

Suddenly it has all gone wrong. *How could I have thought otherwise,* Dahlia thinks. She had hoped to find some common ground with her mother by telling her she and Dudik are through. But it isn't her capitalist son-in-law she hates—it is everything that has not gone precisely *her* way. "Go to hell, Erika."

Zeinab puts down her tray. "My niece!"

Dahlia won't be stopped. "Mother, you are nothing but a heartless communist who loathes her country and even her grandchildren because none of us buys into your stupid, self-hating politics. I might forgive you this, but not how you have enlisted the aid of a woman who—because she had the misfortune to share a birthing room with you—remains loyal beyond all reason. If he hadn't died in battle, my father would today be dead of shame."

"You didn't know your father. He hated injustice."

"I knew him. He hated *you.*" The silence in the room stretches into minutes as Dahlia sips her tea. A crushed mint leaf sits at the bottom of her cup: more fragrance. "Oh, and one more thing: I am giving up my practice."

"As if it does any good."

"To join the Police."

A long pause. "You do everything you can to hurt me."

The Arab woman's face appears to melt. "My dearest niece, I pray Allah will give you strength."

At that moment Dahlia senses the truth: She has come not to bait her mother but to inform the woman who—beyond cause, beyond limitation—has always loved her. "Auntie, if only Allah had made you my mother."

20

Early the next morning on the northern border, Ari leads his three-jeep patrol on a gravel road parallel to the combed-sand security margin. The sand is disked smooth six times a day. Beyond it are three fences, all electrified. Anyone coming over the border and able to get through the fences would have to set foot on the combed sand. Antelope, foxes, wolves, the occasional leopard that does not know it is supposed to be extinct, wild boar, and smaller animals like the highly social hyrax—all of these leave tracks in the sand. When hyraxes travel as many as twenty sets of tracks can be seen, and little else. So every four hours all this natural history is erased. If not, the prints of two-footed predators would be invisible in the tangle of tracks of those with four.

Eyes down, Salim walks slowly ahead, studying for sign.

Ari pulls a pulsing cell phone from his pocket. "Mom, I told you never to call me at the office."

"Save the jokes. Dad told me."

"Whatever took you people so long?"

Ahead of the jeep the tracker stops, circles. He squats down, examining something in the sand.

Ari raises his hand. Yudka stops the vehicle. The jeeps behind halt.

"I wanted to keep the family together."

"Yeah, till the grandchildren are married. Get real, mom. We're fine. We'll *be* fine."

"Uri is just a baby."

"He's seventeen. He called me from school. He's cool. Really." Salim approaches, looking puzzled. "Mom, I got to go."

"Ari, don't be—" It is all he hears. The cell phone is already in his pocket.

"What?"

"I never saw this," the tracker says. "Not in three years in uniform." He holds up a cigarette butt.

"Salim, someone stupid in the morning patrol tossed it."

The tracker shakes his head, pointing to the Arabic calligraphy on the butt. "Liban," he reads. "It's Lebanese."

21

Dahlia is still speaking into her phone as the morning sun glances off the gold-hued Jerusalem stone of the headquarters of the Israel Police, just within the Sheikh Jarrah neighborhood of Arab East Jerusalem. "Ari, don't be a hero," she says. "Be careful." She realizes the line is dead. She drops the phone into her bag.

Entering the six-story building, she shows her ID to the sentry.

22

Ari stands in the jeep, sweeping the fence with his binoculars, searching for breaks. He is looking the wrong way. Heavy automatic fire breaks out from the Israeli side. For a moment he believes it is friendly fire, an error, but in a heartbeat he knows. The machine gunner in the second jeep is already returning fire. Ari leaps out to take cover behind his jeep when an RPG destroys the second vehicle, bodies flying. Almost immediately another RPG takes out the third. Ari's driver takes a shot to the head, his brains spattering the flat windshield like pancake batter. Yudka will never drive for a general, nor will he ever have a girlfriend. He should have been wearing his helmet. They all should be, but the border has been quiet for years.

Ari and the tracker return fire in the direction of the shooting, though neither can see their attackers. They are dug in. It's impossible the enemy could be on the wrong side of the border without disturbing the fences or the sand margin. But there is no time for speculation. As Ari replaces his spent magazine, Salim leaps to the right, screaming in pain. The tracker has been hit in the foot. Somehow a shot got under the jeep. He is now out in the open, exposed from the waist down. The firing stops. Ari tries to reach for the jeep's radio. A burst of automatic fire pings the jeep, then ceases.

An amplified voice, at once melodious and threatening, calls out in English from somewhere in the low bushes south of the gravel road. "Officer in command, please be so kind as to put down your weapon and raise your hands."

For a moment Ari recalls the amplified voice of a lifeguard at the pool in which he learned to swim: *Boy in the red trunks, quit splashing or leave the pool.* Ari is not about to leave the pool. He fires in the direction of the amplified sound.

From his position in ambush, Tawfeek Nur-al-Din raises his megaphone and speaks again. "Commander, surrender and save the life of your tracker, or both of you die here. Do the right thing, commander." He signals to the marksman at his side.

Salim jerks in the air like a marionette, crying out in pain even before Ari hears the shot. It has hit his knee.

Tawfeek Nur-al-Din raises the megaphone to his lips, almost kissing it. "Jew, with intention that missed being a fatal bullet. Shall we have another shot?"

23

A young constable wearing a tight skirt and an Israel Military Industries 9mm pistol shows Dahlia to an office in the second sub-basement.

"This is it?"

"Bomb-proof," the girl says as she leaves. It is meant to be humor.

The room is airless, poured concrete walls left unpainted, a single bulb hanging from the low ceiling over a metal desk holding a phone, a computer keyboard, and a monitor. Behind the desk is a tall gray filing cabinet, rusting in places, drawers open, empty.

Dahlia picks up the phone. Dead. She turns on the computer. The screen requests a code. No one has given her a code. "God help me," she says aloud. She thinks, *For this I gave up my practice?* It occurs to her she has not fully evaluated the price. *For this I gave up my life?* She recalls a cousin, the sole religious one in her secular family, who discovered on her wedding night the groom was not functionally heterosexual. She opens the desk's top drawer: three fat files. *Ah, work.*

She has gotten through the first folder, marking it up in her neat way in a red pen she has brought from home, a good thing, because there is not so much in the desk as a rusty nail to write with.

The file concerns the case of a young Druze from Daliyat al-Carmel, just inland in the hills from her own home in Caesarea. The Druze make up a minority of about a hundred thousand in Israel, practicing a religion that split off from Islam a thousand years before. The community voluntarily undergoes conscription to the IDF, many Druze having risen to leadership positions in the Army and Police. Awkwardly, they have done the same in Lebanon and Syria, where there are even larger concentrations. In a practice known as the border telephone, Druze families who are split by the artifice of lines on a map regularly gather at the Syrian border to call out to each other. The military authorities permit this, not so much as a humanitarian gesture but because the Druze are valued as fighters in both armies. And to gather information.

The file in Dahlia's hands describes a young Druze farmer, one Majid Halabi, a reserve corporal in the IDF, who was caught crossing the border *back* from Syria. He is suspected of working for Syrian intelligence. Investigation has revealed that Halabi is in serious debt, a sign of motive. But according to his written statement what he needs more than money is a wife on whom to spend it, for whom to build a house, with whom to establish a family. Because he is closely related to other members of his clan in Daliyat al-Carmel, he claims to have gone to Syria merely to acquire a bride who is not his cousin. Through the border telephone arrangements were made for him to meet three candidates. According to his statement, more damning than exonerating, he had crossed back and forth three separate times. Though this in itself is enough to guarantee a prison sentence, Police Intelligence is recommending "moderate" extraordinary measures to discover whether his visits to Syria have another dimension. *What,* Dahlia asks herself, *can "moderate" mean? Is there a menu, or does each interrogator follow his own instincts?* There is so much she does not know. She turns back

to the file: It has not been established what, if anything, Halabi was carrying when he crossed over into Syria; in any case, Intelligence questions whether he could have gotten away with the crossings without the cooperation of the Syrian Army or the Mukhabarat, Syria's secret police. Though the border is fenced on both sides, its length over mountainous terrain hardly makes it impregnable—in some spots one can look down on the fence from only a few meters further along the same barrier. Is Halabi a suitor or a spy? Complicating the problem is the vocal Israeli Druze community, which is exerting pressure on the prime minister's office to resolve the matter one way or the other. Dahlia is in the midst of reviewing her own notes when the door opens.

"Nice dungeon."

Without thinking, Dahlia stands. Whoever this is, his insignia indicates he outranks her by two grades, but that is not what draws her to her feet. She is seated in the room's only chair. "Welcome, deputy commissioner."

"Shem-Tov, Kobi," he says crisply, last name first, a practice inherited from the British, who administered what was then Palestine from its capture in World War I to their withdrawal in 1948. Even civilians introduce themselves this way. It often confuses foreigners. Blue eyes, square chin, well over six feet— Dahlia thinks the man looks like an advertisement for the native Israeli, subspecies *militarus professionalis*. He does not look like a cop at all. Even at the highest ranks, like Chaim Zeltzer, Israeli policemen affect a kind of sloppy impermeability. Not here: no slouch, shoulders set back, blue uniform pressed to within a millimeter of perfection. The deputy commissioner's short blond hair is topped by a black-and-white knitted skullcap in a checkerboard pattern that appears to have been hand-crocheted. White ritual fringes dangle down his trousers at the sides. This Orthodox gear normally would be signal enough that Kobi

Shem-Tov is one of those religious men who shield themselves from physical contact with women, and thus from temptation. For the black hats it is absolute—with the crocheted-skullcap crowd one can never be certain. On the other hand, the guy is clean-shaven, which suggests flexibility.

At once, as though reading her mind, he resolves the problem.

She puts out her hand in return. "Dahlia Barr."

His grip is relaxed but firm, the tight flesh of his hand cool. "I know."

"I'm glad someone does."

"You'd be surprised." He grins. "Headquarters considers you a one-woman tsunami. Enjoying your accommodations?"

"I've worked in worse."

"In the Army we call it hazing."

"You're Army?"

"Fresh meat. From Army Intelligence to Police Intelligence."

"Why do *police* and *intelligence* sound like a contradiction in terms?"

"We're improving. I was Zeltzer's big acquisition, until now."

"Ooh, Zeltzer," she said. "Sounds like fun."

"One is subordinate to the rank, not the person. Good commanders are not necessarily pleasant."

"Is Zeltzer a good commander?"

"What do you think?"

"I think he's a piece of shit."

"That's because he doesn't like you. I wouldn't like you either if Zalman Arad had stuck you up my ass."

"Charming."

"Zeltzer's expression, not mine. Meanwhile, I have no intention of descending from the sixth floor to the second sub-basement every time I need to consult with you on matters of interrogation." He smiles. "You appear surprised. In confidence, not to be repeated, it did not take long for me to under

that there are zero rules for what we may call elevated levels of interrogation. Somehow or other Zalman Arad received an unhappy memo to that effect. You are the result. Now kindly stop smiling and pack your papers. I'll show you to your office."

"And what, pray tell, is this?"

"Zeltzer being vindictive. Or just teaching you an early lesson."

"I'm beginning to like you, Kobi."

"That is entirely my intention. It's a bit of a secret, but as a condition of my transfer to the Police I not only demanded your job be created but helped pick you for it. Just because our enemies use torture is no reason we should follow. We're better than that. Directorate meets at fourteen hundred hours." He points to the files on her desk. "Be prepared."

24

At the Lebanese border IDF troops comb the ground. Three armored personnel carriers and a dozen jeeps stand with their motors running. Helicopters hover overhead, above them a single drone transmitting live video to the rear.

A jeep pulls up. A lieutenant colonel, about thirty-five, his face a deep olive, steps swiftly out, removing his sunglasses. He carries a Micro Tavor rifle, one of the first to be issued. Eventually the weapon will replace the Galils and M-16s that are the standard personal weapons of the IDF. The Micro Tavor is not issued to just anyone in khaki.

A young captain disengages himself from the group of even younger officers around him. "Shalom, Gadi," the captain says, recognizing the superior officer at once: Lt. Col. Gadi is a legend whose commando exploits are part of the unwritten lore of the IDF officer corps. Even so, in the IDF officers and enlisted men are called by their first names. Israel remains a first-name society—even in elementary school students call teachers by their first name. The IDF is perhaps the only army in the world where a private will address the chief of staff with easy familiarity, even to the extent of using his nickname. "Yaron, sir. I had no idea you were in this sector—"

"Socialize later. Report."

"We got here twenty minutes after radio contact was suspended. Seven dead. Two jeeps destroyed, RPG, the lead vehicle abandoned, motor still running. Blood on the ground from there through the fences. Ambush point sixty meters south. We found twenty-two hang gliders. Unbelievable, hang gliders."

Gadi points to the first fence.

The young captain nods. "Twenty-three sets of tracks, another set of boots dragged."

Gadi replaces his sunglasses. "Very good, Yaron. Continue searching." He has a mild lisp: *thearching*. "You have about ten minutes before the tanks arrive, after which there won't be a track on the ground that doesn't look like hamburger."

For the briefest moment Gadi wishes his old intelligence officer had remained in the Army. Kobi Shem-Tov had been the best field intel man in the IDF, like himself a veteran of the chief of staff's commando unit. Now where was he? Adjudicating parking tickets? Who would be making these decisions today, some kid fresh out of intelligence school?

"We're going in?"

"Not my decision."

"Request permission to join, sir."

Gadi smiles bleakly. "Yaron . . ."

"Yes, sir."

"Let's leave operational staffing to the brass. You okay with that?"

"Okay, but not happy."

"In this place there's nothing to be happy about. Anything else?"

The young captain looks suddenly sheepish. "I almost forgot." He reaches into his placket pocket. "This was found in the sand."

"A cigarette butt?"

"Not one of ours, sir. Lebanese."

"Clearly. Only one?"

"Where the infiltrators were dug in, near the hang gliders, maybe twenty more."

"In the same spot?"

"In a pile."

"One person, twenty cigarettes. How long does it take to smoke twenty cigarettes?"

"I'm not a smoker, sir."

"It has to be hours. Are there tracks going the other way?"

"None that we could find."

"Yaron, get these men searching a hundred and eighty degrees from the ambush point." Gadi pulls a military cell phone from his chest pocket. "Skull, this is G-One. Requesting a general alert, status red. The entire eastern sector to a depth of twelve kilometers. Full air. We know how many crossed back. We don't know how many stayed behind. I'll remain at the scene." He listens, then snaps it shut.

"Sir, with your permission. There are twenty-two hang gliders. All of these are accounted for."

"How so?"

"Aside from the one prisoner on foot and the other dragged, twenty-two sets of tracks."

"You ever see those videos where a hang glider instructor takes up a trainee?"

"Fuck. We don't know how many actually came over?"

"Exactly. Have your men search for tracks going the other way."

"I'm sorry, Gadi. I—"

"Yaron, is there anything that makes you believe this discussion is not over?"

In the south, a cloud of dust rises as the first units of a tank brigade approach. In a few minutes, the sound will be deafening.

25

In a windowless meeting room, bare but for a large flat-screen on one wall, four officers sit around a conference table. Along with Zeltzer, Kobi, and Dahlia is a darkly intense man wearing thick tinted glasses and an even thicker mustache. He is Chief Supt. Zaid Jumblatt, the highest-ranking Druze in the Israel Police.

Jumblatt smoothes his mustache, first one side, then the other. "So you are saying none of these three are candidates for extraordinary means?"

"None of these *is* a candidate," Dahlia says, not so subtly advancing the case for grammar as well as civil rights. "Two Arab troublemakers, would-be politicians. A university student and a housepainter. We still have free speech in this country."

"There is a difference between free speech and incitement, madam." In not using her rank, Jumblatt is making sure she knows who is the professional. "They incited to riot."

"A demonstration," Dahlia says. "My mother demonstrates every week before the Knesset. For one reason or another, thousands do. It's called democracy."

"With rocks?"

"Chief Supt. Jumblatt, even *if* rocks were thrown—"

"Are you questioning *whether* rocks were thrown? We have six injuries. Chief commissioner, if we don't make an example of these two, we will have twenty more just like them tomorrow, and two hundred more next week. I know these people. They hate us."

Dahlia closes her file. "Hate is not yet a crime in the State of Israel. Pending further information my decision is final. Nobody touches them. Incitement to riot is indeed an offense. In consequence, the matter will be referred to the Office of the State Prosecutor. Our hands will be clean. And that includes the case of the young man who crossed and recrossed the border."

"With all due respect, madam," Jumblatt says, "this is bullshit."

"You're a Druze, chief superintendent. You have relatives in Syria?"

"I don't cross the border illegally."

"There *is* no legal way to cross that border. We are in a state of war with Damascus. The man says he's looking for a wife. According to his file he was found to be in possession of nothing more formidable than an erection."

"Madam, you are new to this—"

"Chief superintendent," Dalia says quietly.

Zaid flashes a reluctant smile. The back of his mouth is largely gold. "Chief superintendent, then. If this bastard is not made an example of, we'll have Druze crossing back and forth like ants at a picnic. In one hour I can know his every secret."

Kobi taps a pencil against the plastic water bottle in front of him. "Change, Zaid. Get used to it. From this point forward, it has been decided by powers higher than those in this room that independent counsel will make any and all decisions regarding enhanced measures. At this moment in the history of the State of Israel that independent counsel is Chief Supt. Barr."

"Three cases," Zeltzer says from the head of the table. "Three negatives. Why am I not surprised?"

Kobi raises his water bottle and sips from it. "With all due respect, Chaim, we have a situation before us that is a bit more urgent. And certainly more grave."

Zeltzer hawks up and spits into his handkerchief. "Brief her."

Kobi picks up the remote control in front of him and kills the lights. "Dahlia, I believe you know this man." The flat-screen comes alive with a head shot of Mohammed Al-Masri. It is the beginning of a slide show: Al-Masri on CNN, Al-Masri with his wife and child at an anti-Israel rally at United Nations Plaza in New York, Al-Masri in the El Al departure lounge at Montreal International Airport, Al-Masri in detention at customs at Ben Gurion Airport. Finally, the suitcase, tan plaid with blue piping.

"Do I know him? Mohammed Al-Masri was a fellow student at Pardes Hanna Agricultural High School. We studied in the same classes."

Zeltzer wipes his lips with the handkerchief. "What sort of Arab goes to school with Jews?"

"An ambitious one," Dahlia says. "Why are we looking at these photos?"

Kobi turns up the lights. "Your friend was stopped at the airport with a suitcase containing the equivalent of one million dollars in euro notes. Give or take."

For a long moment the silence in the room is palpable, a presence all its own. Though Dahlia's face is blank, the face of a veteran defense attorney receiving unwelcome news, her lips become slightly pursed and her eyes narrow. As quickly, she recovers. "I never said he was my friend."

"Certainly no friend of Israel," Kobi says.

"If that were a crime we would have to jail half the world."

"The crime here is currency smuggling," Kobi says.

"Obviously." She does not wish to fight with the only person in this room she likes.

"Less obvious is why," Kobi says.

She turns to him as though they are alone in the room. "How does Al-Masri explain the money?"

"Mr. Al-Masri says it is to build a home for his mother in Baka al-Gharbiya."

Zeltzer comes into it. "Per our chief of intelligence here, you know the mother as well, chief superintendent. She works with your own mother. A peacenik."

"I know Zeinab Al-Masri and hold her in high regard." Dahlia takes a breath. "As a girl, I have on numerous occasions been to her home. She is . . . above reproach."

"Nevertheless," Kobi says, "we do not buy Al-Masri's story."

"It is conceivable," Dahlia hears herself saying. "Arabs do build houses."

"Conceivable but hardly necessary," Kobi says. "Nothing prevents the legal transfer of foreign currency. This was smuggled. Hidden."

"Apparently not very well."

"That is exactly the point, Dahlia. Why hide the money, and why so clumsily?"

She considers. "And why euros? Why not dollars?"

"Only a guess," Kobi says. "The highest denomination American banknote is one hundred dollars. Euros are available in five-hundred-euro notes. To bring in the same value in dollars would require an entire suitcase."

She nods. "Perhaps police and intelligence are no longer mutually exclusive categories."

"Also," Kobi says, "American hundred-dollar bills are widely counterfeited. Thus hard to move. Euros are more sophisticated, with some forty security measures within the surface. Laser printers can duplicate dollars, but not euros. Hence they are more trustworthy and thus universally transferable." He fingers the white ritual fringes that hang out of his trousers. "Many of these subtleties are not widely known."

Dahlia finds herself nodding. "You are suggesting that a professor of political science is unlikely to be aware of them?"

Kobi looks her directly in the eye. "Not without the advice of, let us say, specialists."

"Where is he now?"

Jumblatt leans forward. "He is my guest in this building."

"Since?"

"Last night."

"Forty-eight hours. Then he must go before a judge."

Zeltzer slams his fist on the table. "To bring him before a judge we must admit we hold him. Once that occurs, we send a signal to his accomplices. And to the press. When that happens, he will doubtless get himself a lawyer. Someone like you, chief superintendent."

Dahlia pauses to consider whether this personal attack is worth responding to. "Chief commissioner, the law on secret imprisonment is well established. It is known as habeas corpus. The man is a citizen of the State of Israel. As such he is protected by its laws, just as you are."

Zeltzer's face begins to grow red. "Chief superintendent, with all due respect, I am not a fucking traitor. We gave Al-Masri everything, a free university education even, demanding nothing but that he remain a loyal citizen. While Jewish boys died on the battlefield he was exempt from service. This is how he repays us? Scum!"

"Forty-eight hours."

"I am in command here, chief superintendent. Not you, not Zalman Arad, not even the fucking prime minister."

"The law is the law, chief commissioner."

"In matters of national security the law is wrapping paper.

We will keep this piece of shit until he tells us where the money came from and where it was headed. If he refuses to speak, we *will* take measures. This meeting is terminated."

As they stand, Kobi signals to Dahlia, his right hand palm down at his waist, patting the air: *Be patient.* His left hand twists the white ritual fringes at his side as though praying she will be.

26

In southern Lebanon, over serpentine mountain roads half-hidden by arching cedars, a column of three white vehicles marked UN on all sides and on their roofs makes its way northward. The first two vehicles are closed trucks. Inside the third, an ambulance, a bouncing shaft of sunlight illuminates Ari and Salim hog-tied on the floor, black sacks over their heads. The tracker's leg is bleeding through crude bandages. Two Hezbollah fighters guard them, weapons pointed. Salim moans. A Hezbollah fighter kicks him. It is not even personal.

27

In the basement pistol range at Police Headquarters targets fall as Dahlia, wearing ear protectors, empties a 9mm magazine, then expertly drops the empty and inserts a fresh clip to repeat the exercise.

Kobi stands behind her next to an instructor, who marks a form on a clipboard. Kobi applauds. "Impressive."

Dahlia raises her earmuffs higher on her head. "I'm sorry?"

"Now I know why I want you on my side. Though I could have sworn you're left-handed."

"You notice such things?" She reloads both magazines.

"Part of my job."

"I *am* left-handed."

"You did that with your weak hand?"

"You came here to flatter me?"

"I came here to tell you not to confront Zeltzer. Don't push him into a corner."

"Extraordinary measures is my call."

"Nobody challenges that. Even Zeltzer must come to terms with it. It's not you—it's having someone tell him how to run his organization. He's not a bad man."

"He's fooled me, then."

"Dahlia . . ."

"I've got to finish this. Can we talk later?"

"Love to, but I've been called elsewhere. Either way, there's not a lot of time. Look, I want you to talk to Al-Masri."

She nods as she pulls down her ear protectors, transfers the pistol to her left hand, and resumes shooting. The targets fall with implausible rapidity.

28

OFFICE OF THE PRIME MINISTER
Security Cabinet

Memorandum of Record

Present
The PRIME MINISTER, presiding
BEN-DOV, Carmela, Foreign Minister
AL-SHEIKH, Yarden, Minister of Internal Security
BLUMENTHAL, Shai, Minister of Defense
ADMONI, David, Minister Without Portfolio
ARAD, Zalman, Security Adviser to the PM
ROSCH, Dror, Cabinet Secretary

Invitees
TOLEDANO, Aviv, IDF Chief of Staff
LEVAVI, Rafael, Director-General, Mossad
ZELTZER, Chaim, Chief Commissioner, Israel Police
SHEM-TOV, Kobi, Deputy Chief Commissioner, Israel Police

The Prime Minister
Thank you all for coming. A word to those present for the first time: Nothing of what is said here leaves this room. A transcript will be made public

74

thirty years from the last day of the current year, so that history—not our friends in tomorrow's newspaper—may make its judgment. Before that time, nothing of what is said here will be publicized. Tell your wife—Carmela, in your case, husband—and your career will be terminated. If we must manufacture evidence against you, if it happens that an auto accident occurs, whatever must be done, it will be done. Zero tolerance. Dror?

Dror Rosch, Cabinet Secretary

Thank you, sir. Two subjects on today's agenda: [1] This morning's infiltration of the northern border; [2] The incident of Mohammed Al-Masri. Regarding [1], the PM calls for the report of the Chief of Staff.

Aviv Toledano, IDF Chief of Staff

Sometime before dawn, the border northeast of Avivim was penetrated by a force of at least twenty-two fighters, presumably Hezbollah, utilizing flying devices known as hang gliders, a kind of large kite propelled by wind currents. The enemy force attacked a passing border-inspection patrol, killing seven and taking two prisoners. Within minutes they fled back into Lebanon after shorting the electrified fences and cutting through. The prisoners have been identified as a lieutenant of paratroops, son of a person known to this office, and a Bedouin tracker of the Abu-Aziz. One appears to have been seriously wounded, but which one is not known. Per standing policy, names will not be disclosed to the public until their families have been informed, and perhaps well after. Monitoring of Arab channels has not yielded useful information. To this point, no group has claimed credit for the attack. Finally, there is as yet no certainty that other infiltrators did not deploy south into Israel when the main force returned to

Lebanon. In order to prevent panic, no civilian officials other than those in settlements close to the border have been notified. No suspicious activity has been reported. IDF operations are ongoing.

The Prime Minister
Thank you, Toli. Yarden?

Yarden Al-Sheikh, Minister of Internal Security
If we don't have a follow-up incident tonight or by noon tomorrow, threat level is close to zero. There is simply no reason to infiltrate fighters in this manner unless to provoke havoc or, alternately, a distraction. Either way it is extraordinarily risky for the infiltrators; finding shelter with the civilian population even more so. The number of Arab informants in northern Israel is, in effect, the entire Arab population of northern Israel. Historically, these will rat out their brothers, if only not to have their own loyalty to the state called into question. As well, monetary rewards have proved to be not unhelpful.

David Admoni, Minister Without Portfolio
We have recently had anti-government demonstrations, Alon, that would seem to call into question this loyalty.

Yarden Al-Sheikh, Minister of Internal Security
Jews demonstrate against the government all the time. Should Arabs not? Sheltering an armed infiltrator is another matter. My personal opinion: There are no infiltrators. Not least because one man left behind, if captured, might compromise the cousins' entire infrastructure.

The Prime Minister
Which brings us to these damn kites. Can the border be sealed against them?

THE LIE

Shai Blumenthal, Minister of Defense

We are working on installation of low-altitude radar. Apparently, the Americans have found it successful on their border with Mexico.

Zalman Arad, Security Adviser to the PM

Locking the barn door, are we?

Shai Blumenthal, Minister of Defense

Zalman, may I remind you seven soldiers have been killed and two taken hostage. If the security services envisioned such an operation, I don't recall getting the memo.

The Prime Minister

Gentlemen, please. Shaike, when exactly will defense against this be operational?

Shai Blumenthal, Minister of Defense

Toli?

Aviv Toledano, IDF Chief of Staff

One week. Until then the entire northern border will be manned continuously, one set of eyes every five hundred meters.

Zalman Arad, Security Adviser to the PM

A week?

Aviv Toledano, IDF Chief of Staff

Mr. Adviser, this entails over two hundred sets of portable low-level radar devices, not something you pick up at the corner grocery. These devices are currently being sourced through Washington on an accelerated basis.

David Admoni, Minister Without Portfolio

Do we even know if they work?

Yarden Al-Sheikh, Minister of Internal Security
Perhaps they'll work too well. Couldn't they pick up
hawks, owls? Eagles for sure. Antelope. Antelope
leap three meters high.

David Admoni, Minister Without Portfolio
Yarden may be right. How much difference is there
between the size of a hang glider and an eagle? Will
these radars know one from the other?

The Prime Minister
Toli, your people are aware of such issues?

Aviv Toledano, IDF Chief of Staff
Absolutely, sir. Regarding size sensitivity, I am
informed this is relatively simple to calibrate.
Regarding the similarity in size of eagles vis-à-vis
hang gliders, a secondary visual system will be in
place utilizing drones. In cases of doubt, we will
destroy both terrorists and eagles indiscriminately.

[Laughter.]

The Prime Minister
We'll have the Society for the Protection of Nature
on our heads. Shai, you have something to add?

Shai Blumenthal, Minister of Defense
Mr. Prime Minister, as you can imagine, this will
call for a significant cost in reservists—we estimate
four thousand men per week—plus the unexpected
acquisition cost of the radar devices. Our budget is
already—

The Prime Minister
To be taken up in Thursday's meeting of the finance
committee. Prepare your numbers. Now, since we

are already talking about our friends in Washington . . .

Carmela Ben-Dov, Foreign Minister
The Foreign Ministry envisions no problem with purchase of the radar devices. However, with regard to military action I'm afraid that political considerations indicate any but the most discreet—

Zalman Arad, Security Adviser to the PM
Two of our boys have been kidnapped. You are saying that politics—

Carmela Ben-Dov, Foreign Minister
Zalman, don't fill my mouth with your words. I am saying only that the cabinet must in every case be aware of implications outside the immediate neighborhood. Next week the U.S. president will be in Saudi Arabia, Kuwait, and Bahrain. An invasion of Leb—

Zalman Arad, Security Adviser to the PM
Now who is putting words in mouths? I said something about an invasion? But at the least a surgical operation to remove our boys. Also, it would not hurt to show these beasts we can reach out for them anywhere.

The Prime Minister
Zalman, Zalman. Why is it you portray us as a bunch of pacifists meeting to celebrate the birthday of Mahatma Gandhi? Rafi, when will we have a postal address for such a package?

Rafael Levavi, Director General, Mossad
Mr. Prime Minister, this is a question I have been pressing since we received the original information.

Our best guess at this point is that the hostages will remain in Lebanon. The regime in Damascus is unlikely to risk being found to have them in Syria. Alas, frankly and to our sorrow, to hide two individuals in Lebanon is not a great challenge. We have faced this problem many times before. All I am able to say at this point is that we are working on all fronts: electronic surveillance, eyes on the ground, and informants. So far . . .

The Prime Minister
So far?

Rafael Levavi, Director-General, Mossad
So far, nothing.

The Prime Minister
On this subject only, anything else? All right, then. David, you can add this to your portfolio without portfolios. Let me be clear: Per standing policy, names of the hostages will not be released without my direct authorization. All press contacts on the subject via Minister Admoni, who will immediately establish the appropriate provisional infrastructure. Duvvid?

David Admoni, Minister Without Portfolio
Done.

The Prime Minister
Two minutes left. Dror?

Dror Rosch, Cabinet Secretary
Certainly, sir. It seems early this morning a well-known anti-Israel propagandist, Mohammed Al-Masri, a citizen of Israel resident in Canada, was apprehended entering the country with the equivalent in euros of about one million dollars. In cash.

THE LIE

The Prime Minister

A million Israelis are resident abroad. God willing each should return with such a treasure. Chief commissioner, why is this a problem for the security cabinet?

Chaim Zeltzer, Chief Commissioner, Israel Police

First let me say it is an honor to—

The Prime Minister

Chaim, we have ninety seconds.

Chaim Zeltzer, Chief Commissioner, Israel Police

Certainly. Dep. Comm. Kobi Shem-Tov will brief your honors on the relevant details. Kobi.

Kobi Shem-Tov, Deputy Chief Commissioner, Israel Police

Thank you, chief. In sum, though we have only begun to interview Mr. Al-Masri, it is unlikely this hoard of cash is for the stated purpose of building a house for his mother. Given its poor hiding place, we believe the cash was meant to be discovered. Thus we have a well-known person—I would say even a celebrity— under detention for a crime that was *intended* in some way to embarrass the state. A put-up job. There is some suspicion, given the timing, that today's kidnapping on the border is not unrelated. But the specific nature of the connection, if any, is unknown.

The Prime Minister

Thank you, deputy commissioner. And let me say all of us are pleased that you have brought your expertise from the Army to the Police. We expect to hear more on this subject, and look forward to seeing your face in these premises. Dror?

Dror Rosch, Cabinet Secretary

Today's meeting of the security cabinet is adjourned. Those who are not cabinet members are now asked to leave while the cabinet further discusses these and other matters in informal session. Thank you for attending.

29

In her new office, on the top floor with a view of Arab East Jerusalem, Dahlia answers the phone. "Five minutes?" she says. "No need, I'll find it." The office is done in Israel government modern: a large desk with a figured wood top, two intentionally uncomfortable visitors' chairs, on one wall a framed photo of the current president, an inoffensive hack whose lack of initiative over a long political career discouraged one party or another from exercising its veto on his selection. The man is known to be so indecisive that a popular joke has him dithering between ordering coffee or tea, finally telling the waiter: "Half and half."

The bookcase beneath this portrait stands empty but for a copy of *The Geneva Conventions of 1949, All Protocols,* next to it a four-drawer filing cabinet with no apparent rust, and on the other side a two-seat sofa covered in green leatherette. The walls are painted a rudimentary beige. An ashtray full of butts marked with Dahlia's pale coral lipstick sits on the desk, along with a laptop for which she has been supplied the code, which is *Dahlia Barr* spelled backward, an indication of the sophistication of the Israel Police: At least three reporters have already hacked into the system. The ensuing news articles were thought to be the result of leaks from personnel within the department. In fact, the articles simply revealed a consistent lack of investment in the national police force of the country that leads the world in software development.

Though the building is centrally air-conditioned, a small supplemental unit hums in one window. Whoever specified the building's engineering had not considered that in central Israel, where summer temperatures can reach 115 degrees Fahrenheit, a top-floor office beneath an inadequately insulated roof requires a good deal more cooling than a similar office on the ground floor.

Dahlia assumes the office itself is bugged, taking it for granted and not bothering to look for the device. Usually a decoy bug can be found in the telephone handset, meant to be discovered so as to put off the target from searching further. The phone itself is pink. Until Dahlia had a look at other offices, she assumed this was in honor of her status as one of the few persons of authority whose genitalia are internal. But no, all the phones in the building are pink. Doubtless someone's brother-in-law had a supply of pink phones he needed to unload. The blackout blinds that end a foot above the windowsill might have had a similar provenance, or it could be the same person who specified their length was the one who designed the air-conditioning.

Dahlia checks her makeup, picks up her purse, and goes to find Interview Room 32b, thinking as she walks down the long narrow corridor to the stairs, *This is not my job. My job is to monitor interrogations, not carry them out.* By the time she reaches Interview Room 32b—between rooms 31b and 33b; the building's anonymous architect, doubtless also someone's brother-in-law, cleverly placed 31a and 31c on other floors—Dahlia has reached a somewhat more positive conclusion: As much as she does not wish to interview Mohammed Al-Masri, she at least can be sure the object of the interview will not be subjected to torture. *Except perhaps,* she muses, *by nostalgia.*

30

In the interview room, Dahlia finds two constables standing like statues behind a wheelchair in which is secured a shackled figure with a black bag over his head. "Officers, remove the headgear," she says.

One looks to the other. The bag is removed. Mohammed Al-Masri's eyes squeeze closed at the light. Before they adjust, Dahlia has an opportunity to examine his face. It could use a shave but is otherwise in fair shape, all things considered.

"Dahlia Barr."

"Long time."

"I've been demanding a lawyer since the airport. I expected either none or some hack."

"I regret this treatment, Mohammed."

"Edward."

"I beg your pardon?"

"Edward Al-Masri. That is the name on my Canadian passport. That is the name by which I am known in the West. Can I get some water?"

"Officers?"

One of them opens a plastic bottle of water on the small table.

"Untie him."

"No can do," the constable says. "Protocol."

She takes the bottle and holds it to Al-Masri's lips. More goes down his shirtfront than in his mouth. Patiently she holds the bottle until he shakes his head, *no more*. She turns to the constables. "Now be so kind as to leave us, or is that against protocol as well?"

"Not so long as he's tied."

They shut the door behind them with an eerie finality, as though she and Al-Masri are doomed to be together for eternity, or at least—Dahlia thinks—until the pressure on his bladder determines otherwise.

"Mohammed, I'd like to help you."

"Edward."

"I'm not used to it."

"I am. I didn't call you Dahlia Fine, did I?"

"Admittedly we've both undergone a few changes since high school," she says. "Will you let me help you?"

"Will I let the best-known human rights attorney in Israel represent me? Did you ever take me for a fool?"

"I expected you to say *in Palestine.*"

Al-Masri smiles. "A matter of time."

"Really?"

"Injustice cannot last forever. This thing, this entity you people have created, it's a Potemkin village."

"It looks like this Potemkin village can sentence you to five years for currency smuggling, a good deal more if it turns out the money was intended to promote terror."

"That's what lawyers are for. How long will it take to get me out?"

"Mohammed," she says. "That's a matter of time as well."

"Edward."

"Edward."

"Yes?"

"I think I should tell you: You're making an assumption. I'm not what you think I am."

"A virgin?"

"None of us is. How is your wife? You've a son, no?"

"Let me make this easy for both of us," he says. "We've known each other a long time. Your mother and mine are friends. You were regularly a guest at my mother's table. But at the moment chitchat is not on my agenda. Act like my attorney and get me the fuck out of here."

"Tell me about the money."

"Planted."

"I see."

"Stinking Jews." A smile. "No offense."

"Of course not. Planted?"

"This way I can be silenced. I'm surprised they didn't plant a bomb."

"If you're right, why not a bomb?"

"You're asking me what the fucking Jews are thinking?"

"I'm asking you for the truth, Mohammed. I'm told you said the money is for . . . my auntie. To build a house."

"Ed-ward. I'm a citizen of Canada. And I want to see my ambassador. Can you arrange that?"

"You're a citizen of Israel."

"I renounce it."

"You may do so, but as an attorney I must tell you that your crime was committed as an Israeli, and as an Israeli you will be brought before an Israeli court. If found guilty you will have a good deal of time in which to renounce your citizenship. But not now."

"Plant-ed ev-i-dence."

"You have a family. Help yourself: Don't lie to me."

"Dahlia, I have just spent a day, maybe two days, how can I know, shackled to a concrete floor. I would like to shower, brush my teeth, feel like a human being, not some animal. Can you arrange that?"

"I can try." She allows herself a sigh. "Edward."

31

She finds Kobi in a long room with a dozen desks, large monitors where windows should be, electronic maps on a wall the size of the garage doors in her home in Caesarea, each map subtly pulsing with colored lights. About twenty officers move about purposefully or sit attentively at desks with more monitors, large headsets causing them to look like an otherworldly species wearing the uniform of the Israel Police.

"How can you work in this cold?" she asks.

"Computers prefer the Arctic to the Middle East." He holds up one of the white ritual fringes dangling at his sides. "That's why I wear extra underwear." His smile fades. "How did it go?"

"He thinks I'm his attorney."

"I thought he might. You didn't . . . ?"

"Disillusion him? No."

"I thought you wouldn't."

"It's not terribly ethical."

"Neither is he. I think it's called war."

"We become like them, eh?"

"Only when necessary, Dahlia. It beats torture, no?"

"Unpleasant as it is to admit," she hears herself say, "there is a certain honesty about using . . . extraordinary methods. At least it's direct. It doesn't proclaim to be what it's not."

"Does that mean you'd prefer I turn him over to Jumblatt?"

"Of course not," she says. "I was just . . . musing."

32

High in the mountains of southern Lebanon, the convoy of UN vehicles comes to a halt in the brick courtyard of a Maronite church. Any farther inland, where the United Nations has no mandate, UN markings would cause problems: The Zionist enemy has drones whose precise lenses broadcast live video to intelligence analysts who know exactly where UN vehicles are not supposed to be. The white vehicles have served their purpose.

Purple wisteria climbs the walls of the courtyard. Beyond the walls, thick-trunked olive trees stand like mute witnesses on carved terraces that were ancient in the time of Jesus. Behind the church, shaded by three-hundred-year-old cedars, stands a tall funerary van whose shining black lacquer bears on each side the tri-barred gold cross of the Maronites. The two prisoners are dragged from the ambulance and dumped into the van. It pulls slowly out of the shadows.

Except when the various sects, nationalities, and religions that make up Lebanon declare war on each other—this happens every decade or so—clergy of all stripes are respected by the armed militias as a matter of course. Thus the tri-barred cross, representing the unity of the triune God, is as good as any visa, any passport, any armed escort. Even more so when the symbol is attached to a funerary van. As in any violent society, in Lebanon the dead are respected more than the living.

Within the church, two Maronite priests, one white-bearded, the other younger, clean-shaven, are sprawled in the nave. Neat bullet holes, like stigmata, mark their foreheads. The exit wounds are not so neat.

33

Al-Masri is a new man. Cleaned up, wearing a bright white jumpsuit with the word PRISONER stenciled in red on its back, he sits strapped in his wheelchair with such aplomb it might be a throne.

Once again Dahlia is seated across the table. "Feeling better?"

"Oh, delightful. Now I'm a sanitized prisoner of the Jewish State. They even let me brush my teeth." He displays them. "See? Kissing-sweet."

"Except there's no one here interested in kissing you. Edward, let's not waste more time. I need to know precisely what you told the Police about the intended use of the money."

"What I told them was that the money was for my mother, to build a house—"

"She has quite a nice one now."

"Is that a reason to throw me into a cell?"

"You tell me, Edward."

"Not a very pleasant cell, either."

"Why did you make up such a tale?"

"Who says it's a tale?"

"Those who threw you into the unpleasant cell."

"The money was planted, then. We'll say it was planted."

"Who will?"

"You will, as my attorney."

THE LIE

"You would wish me to lie in court?"

"I would wish you to say what I tell you to say. The lie will be mine. You will simply transmit it. Let them prove the money is mine. Planted."

"Was it?"

"What's the difference?"

"Edward, we were born the same time, in the same hospital, adjacent beds. Your mother is dear to me. I don't want you to suffer."

"For my sake? Or for my mother's?"

"Does it matter? I would like to help, but you must be one hundred percent truthful with me."

"The money was planted. Full stop."

Dahlia opens the door. The two constables are smoking in the hall. "We'll talk again," she says. "Unless you are honest with me, my hands are tied."

The constables begin rolling him out.

"*Your* hands are tied? Dahlia, perhaps you are unaware of the difference between reality and metaphor. Look at my hands, my feet. My entire body in this rolling prison."

"Edward, I can't help if you persist in telling fables. No judge will believe them."

He is shouting now. "Just as no one believes seven hundred thousand Arabs were made homeless by your repugnant Jewish State! Do you really think I owe it honesty?" He is at the door.

"Edward, eight hundred and fifty thousand Jews were at the same time booted out of twelve Arab countries. This isn't CNN. You should consider the truth. The truth is always best."

34

A white Subaru sedan with Israel Police markings moves north on the coastal highway. Its driver is one of the one hundred twenty thousand Ethiopian immigrants, or a child of same, who were rescued from Africa and flown to Israel in the final decades of the twentieth century.

"Can I ask a question, chief super?" the Ethiopian driver asks. Like many Ethiopian Jews, even those born and raised in Israel, his demeanor is respectful to the point of timidity.

Dahlia does not look up from her paperwork. "You just asked."

"Another, then?" The driver is all of twenty-two. He looks even younger.

"Why not, corporal?"

"If you are too busy . . ."

She sighs. "What is the question?"

"Is it true you are the one who defends Arabs? From the newspapers?"

"Do I defend them from the newspapers?"

"I mean the one in the newspapers who defends Arabs."

She is about to say *I am.* "I was."

"How can you be on their side and also on ours?"

"There are no two sides. Just people."

He turns to stare at her.

"Watch the road, corporal."

"The Arabs desire to kill us."

"Some."

"Not all?"

"I don't know. Some. Probably most."

"With all respect, chief super. It seems plain."

"This exit." She picks up her cell phone as it vibrates in her bag.

"Hello, gorgeous."

"Not a good time to talk," she says.

"I'm missing you."

"You should be."

The Subaru turns toward the setting sun down a street of villas.

"When can I see you?"

"Not soon. I'm just arriving home."

In the driveway, Dudik's red BMW is parked alongside an older white Volvo with Army plates. She tries to recall whom Dudik still might know who is regular Army. *Why would Dudik be here with an Army officer? In fact, why would Dudik be here at all?*

"Just arriving home. Sounds so-o-o familiar. Why do I get the feeling you don't want to talk to me?"

"Because I don't. Now is just not a good time."

"Edward Al-Masri."

"What?"

"You know who he is, Dahlia. Atlanta is on my ass. He's a CNN contributor. And he's missing."

"I'm sorry. I don't know anything about it." She snaps the phone shut and exits the car, then turns to the driver. "Tomorrow morning. Seven o'clock. Don't be late." As she walks down the path between flowering plants and small decorative palms, she realizes she does not know his name.

As usual, the front door is unlocked. Even before she steps across the threshold, she senses it: everything in its place, the furniture where it should be, no sign of breakage or disorder. But it is there, so clearly there in the way her husband and son stand as she enters, each of them rising as though pulled upward by invisible strings. "What's going on?"

For once her husband is at a loss for words. "Dahlia . . ."

"What . . . is . . . going . . . on?"

"Mom," Uri says.

"Why is a military car here?" Then she sees them: two officers, a man and a woman, standing by the pool, smoking intensely, their eyes down.

"Mom, it'll be okay."

Later, attempting to recall exactly what happened, she will remember nothing but finding herself in Dudik's arms, a strange feeling. She has not been this close to her husband in five years, maybe longer. After so long, the smell of him is both foreign and comforting: maleness, aftershave, tobacco. He smokes a cigar a day, a big fat Dominican—the name Fuente comes to her suddenly. He smokes Chateau Fuente. But when he travels to the U.S. he always carries a couple of boxes of Havanas. They can't be purchased in the U.S. but are widely available here. The Americans are crazy for Havanas. Abruptly she hears him say, a quote out of better days, "Dominican cigars are better. The Americans are fooling themselves. They desire what they cannot have." She is coming to. He has said nothing of the kind. Not in years. Not now. She is coming to in her own home, and a voice is screaming.

It is hers.

35

In the commercial street below, the chaotic stream of Beirut traffic plunges ahead like a river flowing down from the Litani mountains, now a rapids, now obstructed, now a broad pool. On the sidewalks, women walk holding the hands of children in school uniforms, rucksacks bouncing against their shoulder blades. Shop owners stand still as monuments outside open-fronted stores that will soon be sealed with roll-down steel grates from two to four P.M. and then for the night after seven; none of the shops is fronted with glass. Glass has not worked out all that well in central Beirut. If the glass is not intentionally broken by looters from one militia or another, accidents happen with regularity even in the most placid of neighborhoods, especially accidents involving weaponry. Because Lebanon is only nominally governed, assassination is the traditional method for settling disagreements. Assassinations incite a predictable trail of vengeance killings, which themselves result in an endless chain of reprisals. Even unintentionally, grenades have a way of going off like toxic church bells on their own anarchic schedule. No matter their denomination or agenda, the militias are full of trigger-happy young men with tenuous egos who smoke entirely too much hashish. In these circumstances, even the thickest window glass is not a solution but a problem.

But now the street is peaceful. Older men stop to chat with

shopkeepers they have known for decades, perusing the merchandise, eternal in its lack of variety, that has spilled out amoeba-like onto the sidewalks. The sidewalks are thus narrowed, slowing pedestrian traffic in almost surreal contrast to the manic vehicular traffic only inches away. In the Arab world men do the shopping. Women normally stay home, leaving only to bring their children to school and pick them up, or to socialize with friends, almost always in private homes.

On the opposite side of the street at the rickety wooden tables of a large café, men play dominoes or *shesh besh,* a close relative of backgammon, or read newspapers that only appear to be similar to newspapers published in the West. In the Arab world news is a matter of opinion. Here, newspapers are supported by political parties, each a reflection of the ethnic or ideological makeup of its readership. A few men drink coffee, or mint tea. Most simply sit and converse, or smoke apple- or cherry-flavored Lebanese tobacco through bubbling narghilas. On the rooftops opposite, partly uniformed men in mirrored sunglasses and clothes marked Levi's, Polo, and Abercrombie & Fitch, their fingers caressing the triggers of automatic weapons whose safeties are disengaged, survey the street and the windows of the buildings that line both sides.

In an apartment in a building on this street, Fawaz Awad, newly arrived from Montreal, steps away from the window and takes a seat on one of two ornate divans that face each other, separated only by a large disk-like tray of damascene copper that holds an open cedar box of loose cigarettes. Like the clothes worn by the armed men on the rooftops, the Marlboros and Kents in the box are made in Lebanon for export to other Arab countries where labels count for more than truth. With the dexterity of the one-armed, Awad draws a Gauloise from the pocket of his elegant suit, fits it into his gold cigarette holder, then smoothly lights it with a gold lighter that appears seemingly out of nowhere in his right hand. Even in the strong light of the Beirut afternoon, its flare illuminates the disfigured left side of his face and is further reflected in the gold that frames the lenses of his thick glasses, one of which is blacked out. The effect is both overtly dramatic and quietly threatening. "Where are they?"

Tawfeek Nur-al-Din smokes his own brand, indigenous to Lebanon. Distinctly marked with a stylized cedar tree, the Liban brand is not fake anything, authentic all the more when it is packed with the best hashish the country produces. This Lebanon also exports to the Arab world. Oily, potent, and sweet, Lebanese hash is considered world-class. "Not so very far."

"You won't tell *me*?" With his only hand, Awad brushes a bit of ash off the folded left sleeve of his jacket. "Not even me?"

"Maybe you are working for the Jews." It is both insult and jest.

"Inshallah, then I would be rich."

Tawfeek Nur-al-Din laughs, his richly musical voice making his reply almost a joke. "Then you would be dead."

"If so, you would have no conduit to the old man."

"For what you are being paid, we could place full-page ads in all the Israeli papers. Zalman Arad reads the newspapers, does he not? With the Jews it is an obsession."

"Yes, of course," Awad says. "Wanted to trade: two Israeli soldiers for one Palestinian patriot. Perhaps on the television as well, with jingles. Do you know why we have not wiped them out?"

"Pray tell me, Fawaz Awad."

"We hurt them, but we do not touch them. Bigger and better bombs, missiles, suicide martyrs—if this were the French or the Spaniards, they would collapse at once, the Italians even earlier. But the Jews must be approached differently. If we give them no choice they will fight. However, given choices, they will be compelled to think, to feel. For them the worst situation is moral choice. We must offer them moral choice. Painful choice."

"We shall."

36

Haggard and strung out, Dahlia and Dudik are squeezed into Zalman Arad's narrow office.

"You ask something I cannot give," the old man says.

"We want our son back," Dudik says.

Arad sips tea from his chipped enamel cup. He had offered them tea, but it was declined. He was not insulted. "Welcome to the club of bereaved parents," he says. "Some come to me knowing their son is dead, but they do not accept it. Or ask only for some scrap of information. All of them in the end wish the same thing, that we return their children, or their remains. I give them all the same reply: How can we rescue them if we do not know where they are?"

"You can find them," Dudik says.

"They are moved, sometimes daily. Often we receive information. In Lebanon, there is always someone selling information. Sometimes it is real. More often, like everything else in Lebanon, counterfeit. Or if it is real it is out of date. Our golden rule is simple: If we must expend multiple lives to save a single hostage, so be it, but unless we are sure at least of the location of that hostage, we will not gamble. Right now we know nothing other than that the two lads are gone. And that they are probably alive. For now."

"Can they be bought?"

"This is not Mexico, Dudik. These two boys were not taken for profit. There may be a price, but it will not be money. It will be blood."

Dahlia begins to weep. She has not really stopped since she came home to find the two Army officers. Sometimes the tears abate, but even then she is weeping—in silence, without tears, without so much as a tremor, a constant.

"You were at his bar mitzvah."

"Dahlia, listen to me. You must stop acting like a mother."

"A mother is what I am."

"You must stop acting only like a mother. There are indications the key is in your hands."

"My hands?"

"Mohammed Al-Masri. One can't be sure. But there are signs."

Dahlia straightens her back. She takes Dudik's handkerchief and wipes her eyes. The heavy mascara she favors has long since washed away. "There is no connection other than that he was picked up the same day."

"Dahlia," the old man says, "that Ari has fallen into their hands is happenstance. This could have happened to any of our boys. But it did happen to your son. That Al-Masri has fallen into *your* hands alters the equation."

Dahlia's eyes are dry. "Zalman, are you saying that Al-Masri is somehow related to the kidnapping of two young soldiers? How can that be?"

Zalman Arad rises to indicate the interview is over. "You are asking the wrong person. Ask Mohammed Al-Masri."

37

Later that day, in her office, Kobi lights Dahlia's cigarette. He is the kind of man who carries matches though he does not smoke. "Do you wish to be relieved?"

"Why? Because I'm a woman?"

"Because you're a mother, because you're in pain, because you might better use your strength elsewhere."

"There is no elsewhere. Elsewhere is . . . elsewhere."

"The younger son. You should be with him. And your husband."

"Dudik and I are divorcing."

"He is Ari's father."

Dahlia sighs. "The father is as useless as the mother."

"We'll get through this, Dahlia."

"Zalman Arad believes there may be a connection between Al-Masri and the two boys."

"He may be right."

She stares at him.

"Or wrong. A man like Zalman Arad, he has spent his whole life seeing conspiracy. To a man like that nothing is accidental. To Zalman Arad a pair of mismatched socks is a plot."

"Do you have another idea?"

"Dahlia, I am a trained intelligence officer. Intelligence officers do not have ideas, not least because it is too often difficult to separate one's ideas from one's feelings. The best we can do is deduce from available hard evidence. In this case . . ."

"Yes?"

"In this case we have what is known as proximal data. Two soldiers fell into the hands of the enemy in the same time frame as Al-Masri fell into ours. Coincidence? Normally I would say probably nothing more than that. However, Al-Masri did not merely fall into our hands, he practically leaped."

"Why would he do that?"

"Mind reading is not part of my job description, but as it happens I have in my possession a psychological portrait of our guest."

"I'd like to read it."

"Not more than I would like you to. But this particular document is not for general dissemination."

"Kobi, I am a senior officer."

"And the mother of one of the kidnapped soldiers."

"This somehow precludes my seeing all the evidence?"

"Dahlia, such a document is not evidence. It is psychological conjecture created in less than twenty-fours by a team of professionals whose track record is both admirable and imperfect. How shall I put it?"

"Honestly, I hope."

"Honestly, then. The organization that employs us wishes to know the truth, not to be reassured in its errors. Once you see this speculative report, you are bound to use it to guide your investigation. Your value to me is not your concurrence. It is your independence."

"There's nothing you can tell me?"

Kobi offers a wry smile. "Think of it this way: Some men of action would prefer to be professors. All professors dream of being men of action."

THE LIE

Despite herself, she laughs. It feels so good. "Does this tell me about Mohammed Al-Masri or about Kobi Shem-Tov?"

"Ah," he says. "About Kobi Shem-Tov, I can tell you this: He would rather be sitting on the Riviera or in Rio or Miami Beach, sipping cocktails with little umbrellas in them, a carefree Jew among other carefree Jews, without a nation to protect, without borders to secure, without a care in the world beyond what to choose for dinner. But you know, Dahlia, in the end either we Jews take responsibility for our own fate, or someone else will. And that, the last time, did not turn out very well, did it?"

38

In the basement of the same building where Fawaz Awad and Tawfeek Nur-al-Din sit and smoke, green-uniformed militia drape a cinder-block wall with a green-on-yellow banner marked HEZBOLLAH, out of which one stylized Arabic letter rises like an upstretched arm to hold a rifle. Lighting is adjusted. Armed men discuss shooting angles that do not, at this moment, involve guns. A cameraman in a red-and-white-checked kaffiyeh looks through a viewfinder and directs the straight-backed chair to be moved a bit to the right. "Ah," he says. "Perfection. Just like Hollywood." He smiles. "But with real blood."

39

In the interrogation room Dahlia chain-smokes, staring off into space, and is startled when the door opens and the constables wheel in Al-Masri, his head covered by a black sack.

A moment earlier she checked her face in her compact mirror, then snapped it shut. This is the way Al-Masri looked when first she had seen him in this room, his features so tired they seemed to be a blur, an out-of-focus photo, eyes baggy, skin without luster, mouth so tight it appeared to forbid speech. *There are all kinds of prisons,* she thinks, *but all prisoners are the same.*

"Please remove that thing, officers." When they lift the black sack, Al-Masri clenching his eyes against the light, she dismisses the guards.

"I'm genuinely sorry, Mohammed, about the sack. It seems to be policy."

"Edward."

"Edward."

"Can you do something about my accommodations, then?"

"Bad view?"

"None at all. Don't you think it funny that the world calls the Arabs barbarians?"

"Edward, unless you help me, you can expect to see that view for a long time. Am I making myself clear?"

"Exceedingly."

"Then tell me the truth."

"You know, Dahlia, even in high school, when I wanted to fuck you, I wanted to kill you."

"Your adolescent fantasies are not relevant here."

"You were oh, so . . . good. Such a nice Jewish girl. A volunteer is needed? There is Dahlia. A weak student requires tutoring? There is Dahlia. Every teacher's favorite. And my only competitor."

"Like you, I was ambitious. Ambition took you far, Edward."

"It took me to a prison cell as long and wide as I am tall. They play music day and night. Are you aware?"

"Not Mozart?"

"Heavy metal. Try sleeping through that. Do you know about the lights?"

"I imagine they are bright."

"Bright, on, off, to a rhythm that makes no sense. Day, night—who knows? What day is it?"

"Wednesday."

"Should I believe you?"

"Why should I lie?"

"Because you're not working for me, are you? You're working for them."

"You're delirious. Edward, I'm here to help you."

"I don't trust you. I didn't trust you then. I saw through you. You didn't care about the dumb student who couldn't handle algebra. When you volunteered to clean up the lunchroom after a party, you had your own agenda. And when you resisted my advances—"

"Edward, for heaven's sake. High school? You are charged with a serious crime. Do you really wish to spend the little time we have to discuss my rejecting you when we were—what— sixteen?"

"In my room with no view, with the lights going on and off, the heavy metal, my mind went back to those days. I thought, *Who is this Dahlia that represents me?* I recalled what you told me then, that you were not interested in boys. But you lied. You were not involved with any boy at school, I knew that, but I knew, I know in my heart, that you lied."

She lights another cigarette.

"It was because I am an Arab, a filthy Arab from Baka al-Gharbiya."

"It was because you were a boy, and not a particularly attractive one. I was already a woman. I was interested in men."

"It was because I am an Arab."

"Edward, you are an Arab idiot. I'm no longer sure I want to help you. If it were not for your mother . . ."

"Fuck that! And fuck you, too!"

"Very nice. *Edward.*"

"I wish a new attorney. An Arab."

"And Israel wishes only to live in peace. We don't always get what we wish, do we?"

"I don't trust you."

She grinds out her cigarette. "Well, at least your instincts are sound. I need to know everything about your visit to Israel. Who sent you? Why? And the purpose of the money. I need the truth."

He spits in her face.

She slaps him so hard his wheelchair topples. She wipes her face, calls the guards.

As they right the wheelchair and turn it toward the door, he swivels his head in rage. "A whore then, a whore now!" The rest is muffled. The black sack is thick, double-lined, a barrier to sound as well as sight.

40

Outside the Bedouin tent goats and sheep bleat in a rough enclosure of acacia branches, more or less the only tree capable of surviving in the Negev. To these branches are tied bits and pieces of timber scavenged from the nearby Jewish villages, as well as entire eucalyptus saplings uprooted from roadside plantings. Only steps from where Dahlia's Ethiopian driver dozes at the wheel of her police vehicle, a small gray Arabian mare is tethered to the rusting carcass of a pickup truck with neither engine nor wheels. In the distance are more black tents, beyond which is nothing but cracked brown earth with here and there a camel searching for the odd green shoot.

Dahlia had turned to Kobi to find Salim's family. Bedouin move about, sometimes over hundreds of miles. But in an Israel in which every citizen has a cell phone the Bedouin are no exception. Though there is no public directory of mobile numbers, Kobi's people came up with the right one immediately, and then provided a turn-by-turn map, the last several turns signified by little more than a left by the large rock and a right by the acacia tree split by lightning. The last several miles were little more than goat paths.

Within the tent, a battery-powered radio blares the songs of Umm Kulthum, the great Egyptian contralto of the previous century whose keening songs remain a daily staple on Radio

Cairo, which can be picked up here in the Negev Desert as readily as any station broadcasting from Tel Aviv.

Dahlia, Dudik, and Uri sit cross-legged on rugs in a circle with a wizened Bedouin and his male relatives. Their women, faces tattooed with tribal markings, clear away a huge platter of lamb from the center, serve coffee, then take their places outside the circle. This is a cultural adjustment to the equality of Jewish women in Israel—in other Middle Eastern countries Bedouin females serve and are gone.

As well, in other Middle Eastern countries, a Jewish family would not initiate a visit to a Bedouin family in a gesture of solidarity. With the exception of a dozen here and a handful there, there are no longer any Jewish families in the Arab world. With the declaration of the Jewish State in 1948, they had been driven out.

"My family is deeply honored that you have come to share with us our burden," Sheikh Adnan intones. His Hebrew carries with it the reflective poetry of Arabic, a muted singsong rather than a declarative statement. "Inshallah, the next time, let it be upon a happier occasion."

"Inshallah," Dudik says with a certain awareness that he must take on the role of speaker for his family. *For the first time,* he thinks, *my wife knows her place.* Immediately, he is overcome by shame. *This is not the occasion for stupid macho jokes. Our marriage broke up not because Dahlia did not know her place, but because I did not know mine. Perhaps if we were still together, this thing with Ari would never have happened. No,* he thinks, *that's cheap guilt talking. If I'm going to feel guilty, it had better be of the expensive sort.*

"And this is the younger son? Soon in the Army?"

"Soon, *ya'hawadja.*" It is an Arabic honorific: *gentleman.*

"Please, I am merely a small sheikh. In the Army, they called me Adnan. Master Sgt. Addy. Please tell me what you know."

As is common, they have been eating for an hour without

discussing the reason they are here. As T. E. Lawrence wrote, "By three sides is the Arab way across a square."

"We know as little as you do, Sheikh Adnan."

"Two officers came," Adnan says. It is quite as if he is retelling a legend. "We thought the worst. But a prisoner, this leaves hope. The officers called it a window of hope. Alas, as you can see, we have none. In our tents, the window is not known. Therefore we have windowless hope."

Dahlia decides to speak. Most of her clients are Arabs, though the culture of settled Arabs is distinct from that of the Bedouin—each group despises the other. "You have a multitude of sons, Sheikh Adnan?"

"Eleven. Also daughters. But not with this." He nods discreetly toward one of the women, the youngest. "With this, only the one." He shrugs. "You have seen the other tents?"

"Other wives?"

"Praise Allah, with no offense, we are unlike the Jews. However, all the sons of my wives serve. Trackers, each one of them." He taps his temple. "Myself, thirty-two years I served. In recognition of this service I was presented with a house in a new village near Beersheba." He points, his finger rising in small circles. "What can a Bedu do with a house? The wives fought. The children fought. Even the goats fought. Our neighbors were too close. For us, this is unnatural. We are suited to tents. Some Bedu, they wish to be like village Arabs. Or Jews." Now he glances at the young wife, at once recognition and rebuke. "When we sign to serve in the Army, we men understand there are risks. It is harder for a female. It is the pain of the mother."

Soundlessly the woman rises and whispers in his ear.

"What does she say?" Dahlia asks.

"She says, 'Praise Allah, when those are found who took my Salim, please tell our soldiers to carve out their eyes and kindly fill the bloody sockets with their testicles.'"

41

In the makeshift basement television studio, the star of the moment is being strapped into a chair. Earlier, a doctor saw to the tracker's leg, flooding it with anti-inflammatory medicine and injecting antibiotics. Casually he informed Salim that the knee is lost. "It will no longer be a joint," he said. "It will never again bend."

Once the tracker is secured, a Hezbollah fighter turned stagehand runs lines from an automobile battery to the tracker's bare feet.

Salim is sweating but defiant. "Fuck you all!"

"Traitor," Tawfeek Nur-al-Din tells him calmly. "The world will see what happens to a false Muslim."

"Fuck you all and all your families!"

"Camera."

At the first jolt, the tracker throws all his weight backward as he screams in pain. The chair falls.

"Did no one secure the chair?"

There is the usual discussion among Arabs about who is to blame, then about what must be done, then about why that will not work, then about who should lie on the floor behind the chair and hold it steady. All are reluctant to hold the chair because of the current. The director, once an engineering student before—as he likes to say—God found him, calms these fears with an explanation of the principles of electrodynamics. Also, the chair holder will not be in the picture because the viewfinder is focused only above the traitor's waist. Through all of this, the tracker has moved into a semiconscious state, foam seeping through his clenched teeth. Only when they attempt another take does his jaw abruptly relax, the foam, now pink, flowing freely down his jaw.

42

In the Subaru sedan the family sits in silence, Dudik and Uri in the rear, as the white car stops and goes in the evening traffic that chokes the Geha Road running north along the eastern border of Tel Aviv. They are stuck behind a green Egged bus and ahead of a Goldstar beer truck. As far as can be seen, the road is one long parking lot.

Dahlia checks her watch. "Have we ever used the siren, Elias?"

"No, chief super."

"Let's see if it works."

The *wa-wa-wa* of the siren and the flashing lights cause the Egged bus to edge off the road onto the shoulder, but even as it clears the way, it is evident they will have to wait until a thousand more vehicles do the same.

"Chief super, there is another way."

"Have you ever done it?"

"Only in training."

"Then you need the practice."

"I beg your pardon, chief super?"

"You need the practice. Do it."

Elias turns the wheel hard right around the bus, then spins it back left as the car flies down the shoulder. Between the siren and the sound of the tires on gravel, the noise in the car is deafening. This merely inspires the Ethiopian to shout. "A question, chief super!"

"Go ahead, Elias."

"My family dreamed of coming to Israel! When we learned this was possible, not just a dream, we walked seven hundred miles across all of Ethiopia to Kenya, where the airplanes took us! Of ten of us, six survived! A lion killed my sister! The others, human lions! Now every day we see the television news! War without end! We go to funerals! Our paradise is spoiled! It is very sad for us!"

"For all of us!"

Suddenly the gravel shoulder turns to pavement. They no longer need to shout.

But Elias has gotten used to it. "Why must it be so?!"

"I don't know," Dahlia says softly. "It's a tough neighborhood."

Uri leans forward from the rear. "We have to do something, mom."

"We will, Uri." Her phone buzzes in her bag. She looks at the number, shuts it off. "We will, my darling. We will."

43

In the makeshift television studio the doctor examines Salim once again. The doctor is not Hezbollah but a volunteer. Earlier that day, three Hezbollah entered his office, put a gun to his head, and volunteered his services. He tried to explain that he is a dermatologist. The militiamen had been ordered to bring a doctor. They asked, "Is a dermatologist not a doctor?" Now, with his patient out of his head mouthing a senseless monologue, something about a mare, he does his best. The thing that he most wishes to avoid is to lose this patient. "Keep his head elevated," he tells the Hezbollah commander. "Otherwise he will choke on his own vomit. And keep him warm." He is a dermatologist, for God's sake, who has not looked beyond skin for twenty years. But they, the armed men in the basement, they are the Party of God.

Tawfeek Nur-al-Din places his hand on the doctor's shoulder. "You will stay with us," he says, leaving no room for doubt. "What is required for both prisoners, write it down, and you will have it. These boys must not die."

The commander's use of the term *boys* seems to indicate a sympathetic streak, one that may be appealed to. "What *I* need is to be with my wife and family. They do not know where—"

Before the dermatologist can finish the sentence, the man they call Commander Tawfeek hits him in the face with the butt of his rifle, breaking his nose. Blood flows freely.

"You are a physician," the commander says. "Treat yourself."

44

On the sixth floor Dahlia can find neither Zeltzer nor Kobi, but farther down the hallway she discovers Zaid Jumblatt in his office. She stands by the door. Next to the flat-screen television mounted on the wall opposite his desk is a sepia-tinted portrait of Theodor Herzl, the founder of political Zionism. "Working late?"

"We Druze are not shirkers."

"That is your reputation."

"When you are a minority, you must be twice as good, work twice as hard, three times as long. Come in."

Dahlia tosses a folded sheet on his desk. "Is this what you wanted?"

Jumblatt examines the paper. "It was. But now it is no longer sufficient."

"You requested approval for extraordinary measures. You have it."

"Zeltzer gave orders."

"Chaim Zeltzer has no authority in this area."

"On the contrary. Only Dahlia Barr may permit an extraordinary act, but only Zeltzer may order it carried out."

"We have Al-Masri only a few hours longer."

"Extended. Kobi went to the Supreme Court. Another forty-eight."

"Without my knowledge?"

Jumblatt removes the steel-framed spectacles whose tinted lenses protect his eyes from those of others. His eyes are red, tired. "You have been away," he says softly.

"So?"

He picks up the remote control on his desk. "So it is unlikely you have seen this."

Dahlia finds herself looking down at the remote, as if the issue is this slim bit of electronics encased in plastic. "I don't understand."

"An intercepted transmission. By morning Al-Jazeera will display it to the world. Otherwise we would keep it from you." He fingers the remote. "Regrettably, it has fallen to me to bring you this news." On the opposite wall the flat-screen lights up as tinny Arabic martial music booms out.

Dahlia blanches at what she sees.

"They are working on the Bedu because they believe harming your son will anger the Israeli public. They are racist so they believe we are as well. Dahlia, they will keep your son safe."

"That poor boy," she says, though it is unclear which of the two she means. Later, when told what she said, she herself will not be sure.

45

Escorted by four Cyprus Police motorcycles, a black Ford SUV flying the United States flag on its right front fender comes to a halt before the American embassy in a residential suburb of Nicosia. Cyprus is literally an island of neutrality in the Middle East—in most of which flying the U.S. flag on a vehicle would not be a good idea. Even so, two Israeli security guards in aviator glasses and ill-fitting blue blazers step out of the vehicle to check the empty street. They give an extra look at the windows of the neighboring Greek Orthodox monastery, which happens to own the land on which the embassy stands. Only then does one of the security guards open the left rear door.

A small older man steps out. He wears fifties-era round sunglasses, a sixties-era blue suit, and a new gray tie. Entering the building—which like some outsize mausoleum is faced with limestone inside and out—he is greeted by the embassy's chargé d'affaires, a well-dressed bureaucrat whose shoes are polished to mirror brightness, and a thick individual with a goatee and thinning hair who is officially the embassy's deputy commercial attaché. The Marine guard in the reception booth stands as still as a tree. Whatever it is he sees is not something he will ever consider remembering, unless in a moment of alcohol-fueled effusion he whispers it to his Cypriot girlfriend, who may then whisper it to someone else.

Following diplomatic protocol, the chargé speaks first. "Welcome to Cyprus, Mr. Arad. It's always good to see you."

"Likewise, sir," Zalman Arad says in the clipped accent he acquired in his youth when the British ruled Palestine and Cyprus and much of the Middle East. He follows a protocol of his own. "And this must be Mr. Smith."

"Delighted to make your acquaintance, sir," Smith says. He has been to Tel Aviv twelve times to sit down with Arad and share intelligence of a distinctly non-commercial nature, but protocol is protocol. "Our guest has already arrived."

"Oh, very good," Arad says.

Smith leads him through the magnetometer, which issues not so much as a peep, and up the limestone stairs to a reception room richly paneled in walnut. "Mr. Awad," Smith says. "I believe you know Mr. Arad." He smiles. "It occurs to me—your names differ by only one letter. Funny, I never noticed."

"That is because we are cousins, Mr. Smith," Zalman Arad says. "I do thank you for making available this very pleasant venue."

The hint is not lost on Mr. Smith.

Now that they are alone the cousins do not shake hands. They are of course not alone at all: cameras and microphones record their every gesture, every syllable.

Arad takes a seat on a white linen couch opposite Fawaz Awad, himself seated on an identical white linen couch. Between them a plush white rug is emblazoned with the great seal of the United States of America, an eagle in a circle inscribed with the words *E Pluribus Unum.*

With one-armed grace, Fawaz Awad lights the Gauloise in his gold cigarette holder. "Always a pleasure to see you, Zalman," he says in English.

The older man responds in Arabic. "How I wish I could say the same." He pauses. "Of course you are aware the Americans forbid smoking in their buildings."

"Very health-conscious, the Americans," Awad returns in Arabic. Why not? The Jew's Arabic is perfect. "Admirable. If they are so interested in saving lives, they should not send their sons to die in Muslim lands."

"Not to worry. They will continue to do so." Arad watches as the other man smokes, very much aware of the first rule of negotiation among Arabs: Never speak first. But Zalman Arad has been doing this for a long time. He is unafraid of breaking the rules of negotiating with Arabs. He made most of them. "Fawaz, now that you have sent a message to our hosts, can we speak candidly?"

"As candidly as possible in a bugged room. How are you, Zalman?"

"Exhausted. Almost sixty years I have been at this. It is time to pass the baton. And you?"

"Nothing personal, but I will not retire from service until the last Jew is drowned in the sea." He smiles. "Patience is an Arab virtue."

"How pleasant that you have at least one. You requested this meeting. Here I am."

"Always direct, Zalman. So very Jewish."

"My plane leaves in an hour."

"Then hear me well. In the past, we have bargained over prisoners. You have jailed thousands of our brave fighters, our heroes."

"Suicide bombers, terrorists, murderers of children." Arad offers a wry smile. "Nothing personal. Please do continue."

"Sometimes you have agreed to trade hundreds of our people for one of your own."

"Not I. My government. I would not have traded, not once."

"Now we wish to offer a trade of a different proportion. One of ours for two of yours. Give us Mohammed Al-Masri and take back the two soldiers." He drops cigarette ash on the rug, looks at the Jew, and shrugs. "No smoking, therefore no ashtray. Your American friends, so naive." A pause. "That is the deal."

"Interesting," Arad says. "Who is Mohammed Al-Masri?"

"Please, Zalman. Your plane."

"So you wish only this simple trade?"

"On the Lebanon-Israel border. In daylight. On our side the press will be invited. On yours you may do as you please."

"Why?"

"Because you control your side of the border. If only for a time. The Christian Crusaders did the same. Also temporarily."

Arad is patient. "Why this trade?"

"I'm sure you can draw your own conclusions, Zalman. But if I must I will spell it out. In the past the world came to believe that one Jew is worth a thousand Muslims. Today we wish to correct this misconception."

"One Muslim is worth two Jews."

"Exactly."

"And if my government does not agree?"

"Then, my friend, the two young Jews will suffer."

"I am not your friend."

"Nevertheless, they will suffer."

"And if it happens that your Muslim—his name again?"

"Al-Masri. Quite a famous Muslim. I am surprised that you are not aware of his presence in your dungeons."

"And if it happens as a consequence that this quite famous Muslim suffers as well?"

"My dear fellow, we do not, as the Americans say, give a shit." He removes the lit butt from his cigarette holder, drops it on the great seal, grinds it in with his shoe. "You may boil him in oil for all I care. His value is symbolic." Another pause. "May I offer a piece of advice? If you do not make this trade, in my estimation it will further split your nation. There will be demonstrations in the streets. Perhaps a more reasonable government will be elected. A more pliant one. The electorate will demand you act humanely, that you return these poor young Jews—"

"One is an Arab, in fact."

"Bedouin trash. He wears your uniform, ipso facto he is a Jew." With the same smooth one-handed grace Awad stuffs another Gauloise into the gold cigarette holder and lights up with a motion so fluid it appears simply to occur as a consequence. "The Jews of Israel will demand the return of these two poor soldiers to their parents."

"Which will only tempt your people to kidnap others."

"Exactly." The Arab takes a long drag on his Gauloise. "Did you know, Zalman, that chess is an Islamic invention?"

Zalman seems to be studying the butt as it burns a black hole in the white carpet. He looks up. "Not quite. Invented in India, perfected in Persia, both well before the birth of Mohammed."

"Another Jewish lie."

"Believe what you will, Fawaz Awad. Self-deception is an Arab affliction."

"Nevertheless, we do hold the two soldiers. In this game of chess, you should consider that *check*."

Arad carefully removes his round-framed sunglasses and proceeds to clean them with his handkerchief. "Nevertheless, Fawaz Awad, *you* should consider Falkbeer, Loewenthal, Steinitz, Tarrasch, Zukertort, Tartakower, and Lasker."

"Who are these?"

"Also Rubenstein, Nimzowitsch, Breyer, Spielmann, Reti, Botvinnik, Reshevsky, Fine, Horowitz, Boleslavsky, Bronstein."

"What are these names to me?"

"Jewish chess champions. Grand masters. Did I mention Averbach, Najdorf, Smyslov, Polugaevsky, Tal, Geller, Fisher, Timanov, Korchnoi, Stein?"

"Your point?"

"And of course Kasparov, Polgar, Svidler, Radjabov, Gelfand.

My memory is not what it was. I may have missed one or two. All Jews. Tell me, Fawaz, how many Arab chess masters can you name?" Abruptly, he stands. "The next move, sir, is ours." He smiles, the ends of his lips curling up but his eyes remaining as they were. "And do take care with your cigarettes," he says in English. "You could start a fire."

46

Outside the Knesset building mounted police restrain two separate crowds.

On one side of the plaza about two dozen demonstrators hold placards that read BOMB HEZBOLLAH! and NEVER AGAIN! On the other side Erika and Zeinab—with placards that say JEWISH & ARAB CITIZENS FOR PEACE and NO POLICE STATE!—lead about fifty people chanting the same. These are the famous Citizens in Black, for decades a radical thorn in the side of every Israeli government, whether right, centrist, or insufficiently left. The press is out in force, most—revealing a certain political tendency on the part of the international media—behind the barrier restraining the Citizens in Black.

To the rear of that group Floyd Hooper stands with a stylishly dressed blond woman wearing on her shoulders the red-and-white kaffiyeh identified with the Palestinian cause. On Genevieve Al-Masri the kaffiyeh is as much a fashionable accessory as a statement of political identification. She holds her crying toddler, whom she attempts to comfort. With his back to the demonstrators, who face not the hand-hammered wrought-iron Knesset gates but the opposition, Hooper stands before the Steadicam held by his cameraman and speaks directly into the microphone in his left hand, and thus indirectly to the CNN newsroom in Atlanta. Any other kind of microphone would pick up too much of the tumult around him and drown him out.

"Wolf, I'm here with Genevieve Al-Masri, wife of missing Palestinian spokesman and frequent CNN contributor Edward Al-Masri, who was last seen detained at Israel Customs when he flew into Jerusalem on Sunday from his home in Canada. According to CNN sources with ties to the Palestinian leadership, Al-Masri, a professor at McGill University in Montreal who holds dual Canadian-Israeli nationality, is being held by Israeli security forces. Israel government officials have declined to comment. Mrs. Al-Masri and the couple's young son have flown here from their home in Montreal to discover the truth of her husband's whereabouts." He turns to her. "Genevieve Al-Masri, what do you think has happened to your husband?"

"I wish I knew," she says in a French-Canadian accent that would be charming were she not clearly angry. "All we do know is that he's missing. Israeli officials won't tell us where he is, whether they have him in custody, or whether he's even alive."

"What makes you convinced he's being held by Israel? Couldn't your husband be in hiding?"

"From whom? He was last seen at Ben Gurion Airport. Then he vanished." Now her voice rises in pitch, as though she is reciting from a prepared text. "It is no secret that the Israelis have been trying to silence Edward from telling the truth about the Palestinian holocaust. I warned him not to go to Israel, but his family is here. He came to write a book documenting the ethnic cleansing of his people. Now the Israelis have him."

"Mrs. Al-Masri, what's your next step?"

"I want my husband back. Our son needs his father. Later this evening I expect to meet with the Canadian ambassador to enlist his aid. The Israelis can't simply pick up a Canadian citizen and hold him incommunicado. Not even the Nazis went so far."

"Mrs. Al-Masri, according to CNN sources, a possible exchange is being discussed: your husband for the two IDF soldiers captured the very same day he arrived in Israel. As you know, Hezbollah claims the two soldiers were taken in response to his arrest. Has anyone in authority confirmed that a trade is being negotiated, or even envisaged?"

"I hope and pray such a trade is in process, but no one has informed me one way or the other. Failing such an outcome, I will bring this outrage before the High Court of Justice in The Hague. The time has come to put a stop to Israel's trampling on the human rights of the Palestinian people, whether in the conquered territories or within Israel itself."

"Thank you, Genevieve Al-Masri, wife of Palestinian spokesman Edward Al-Masri, whose name viewers will recognize as that of a frequent CNN commentator on the subject of Palestine." The correspondent is in motion, his cameraman following. "I am now walking over to the leadership of today's protest outside the Knesset, Israel's parliament." Abruptly, his way is blocked by a mounted policeman. "Now, if I can get through, perhaps we can have a word with Edward Al-Masri's mother, Zeinab Al-Masri, one of the leaders of the joint Jewish-Muslim peace movement known as Citizens in Black."

The mounted policeman holds his ground, the tall sorrel horse a snorting, high-stepping barrier. "You must go back!"

"I'm with CNN. Press."

"Go back!"

"Look, I just want to—"

The mounted cop is not about to engage in a discussion. He edges his mount sideways so that its advancing flank forces Hooper to edge back.

"You can't do this!" Hooper shouts into his microphone, addressing his audience of millions as well as the mounted cop. "I'm press!"

47

At their villa in Caesarea, three members of the Barr family watch the confrontation on CNN. Seated between them, Dahlia takes the hands of her husband and son.

On the television screen, Hooper has taken up a new position at the rear of the left-wing demonstrators. With the aplomb of a seasoned correspondent he gestures broadly behind him. "So that's the situation from Jerusalem, Wolf. One group calling for justice—in this case, the release of Edward Al-Masri, believed to be held by the Israeli security services—the other side calling for war against Hezbollah, the Lebanese-based Palestinian freedom fighters whose militia claims to hold two Israeli soldiers captured on the northern border." He leans forward, trying to hear what Atlanta is saying.

On the television screen, the unflappable news anchor in Atlanta, whom few viewers know was a longtime correspondent for *The Jerusalem Post* but whose political leanings are now less predictable, picks up the thread without missing a beat. "Hoop, so you're saying no one knows definitively if Prof. Al-Masri is indeed being held by Israel?"

"That's right. But generally reliable Palestinian sources we have spoken with do regard this as fact."

"And the two Israeli soldiers?"

"Wolf, we know almost as little, not even their names, which have not been released. However, a spokesman for the Israel Defense Forces confirmed earlier today that the two were most probably taken prisoner by Hezbollah."

"Thank you, Hoop. That was CNN Mideast bureau chief Floyd Hooper live from Jerusalem. Meanwhile, CNN has obtained a chilling video from Hezbollah in Lebanon. Sources in the Washington security establishment believe it to be genuine. Though CNN has edited this footage for content that is not suited to a general audience, viewers are cautioned that what you are about to see does contain scenes that—"

Dahlia puts down the remote as the screen goes black. "I don't want it shown. Not in this house."

48

At the same moment, Tawfeek Nur-al-Din and Fawaz Awad are also watching CNN, which has become the lens through which either side in any international conflict evaluates its success in convincing the world that it is completely in the right. Fawaz Awad puffs on the Gauloise in his gold cigarette holder, the Hezbollah commander smokes the same Liban brand found in a pile of twenty at the ambush point on the other side of the Israeli border. Butts overflow the large brass ashtray between the two men. From outside the apartment comes the sound of early evening automobile traffic and the occasional hoarse cough of a truck grinding its gears. Militiamen coming on duty at several choke points just to the east have already begun to limit access to the street. When no vehicles pass, the sound of dominoes being slapped down can be heard from the café across the street.

"What did I promise?" Fawaz Awad says. "Even according to the CNN, it is check."

"Not every check leads to mate."

"This one is guaranteed. In Nicosia I saw the old man's face. He is tired. They are all tired."

"But you say yourself he is not the decider, only the adviser. The Jews' internal politics will cast the final vote."

"That is as I have told you. If it were up to the old man, we could capture his own son and no exchange would be made."

THE LIE

"He lost this son years ago, so this is simply an unprovable theorem."

"Regardless, the internal politics of the Jews works against him. He is not only tired but helpless. It is the weakness of democracy. The Jews are sentimental for their children. And in the war room of public opinion, sentiment will always win out. It is all over but the Jewish disappointment. This check will be mate."

"You think it is over?"

"I know it."

"With the Jews, it is never over."

"Damn the CNN—they have edited out the best parts."

"They are in league with the Jews. The Jews control everything."

49

At the same moment, on the damp cement floor of a basement in a bombed-out building only minutes away, Ari rocks the tracker cradled in his arms. The Bedouin is delirious, muttering incomprehensibly, though from time to time Ari makes out the word *mare* in Arabic and the phrase *no more.*

"What color is the mare, Salim?" Ari keeps asking as he rocks him in his arms. "Tell me, what color is the mare?"

50

Dahlia does not want to leave Uri but Dudik is there in the home he had only days before left for good. Uri is not going to school. His father is not going to the office. Neither of them is able to do anything but wait. Dahlia cannot wait.

Speeding through and around the early morning traffic on the coastal road, Elias drives with his teeth clenched, riding the horn when the siren alone is insufficient to clear the highway. In the front passenger seat Dahlia concentrates on nothing but the road, and then shuts her eyes so as not to see it at all. *Elias has his job,* she thinks. *And I have mine.*

She has moved into an almost unconscious state, a state of rest in preparation for the battle ahead, when she hears the cell phone buzzing in her bag. She does not bother to read who the caller is. She knows. "Yes?"

"I love it when you talk dirty."

She thinks, *So the names have not been made public.* "Wait one minute." She has Elias pull over. Who knows how much English the driver knows. She steps away from the car. The noise of traffic is like an assault. "Floyd . . ."

"How is it going with Al-Masri?"

"I don't have a clue," she says. "And if I did, I wouldn't say. Darling, I'm not a source for information on this. Anything you need to know about your colleague Al-Masri will have to come from somewhere else."

"I never met the man," he says. "Look, I need to see you."

"Please don't be offended, Floyd, but I'm not able to see you, not now."

"I was thinking maybe I can help about . . . a related matter."

She is silent.

"Something you might be able to pass on. I've been talking to our guy in a certain city north of here. Begins with a *B*." No response. "Dahlia?"

"I'm listening."

"This isn't something for the phone."

"I understand."

"If you can't come to Jerusalem, I can be in Tel Aviv."

"Five o'clock. Jaffa. You know where."

"I'll be there."

"One thing," she says.

"I'm listening."

"If this is just a ploy to see me, you'll never see me again."

"Five o'clock is a long time off," he says. "It would be good to know who the soldiers are. I can be way out ahead on this. It'll be helpful."

"I can't give you this information," she says. "Is that all you want?"

"I told you. I had a word with our guy in . . . that place. It might be useful."

"And you want something in return."

"It's not quid pro quo. I just thought, if you could get the names . . ."

"Floyd, go fuck yourself."

"It's so much more fun with you."

She softens. *He doesn't know. I can't blame him for that.* Often when they arranged to meet, they went through this same small burlesque. She would say, *But how will I know you?* And he would say, *Extremely attractive, black T-shirt, safari jacket, hard-on.* And she would reply, *I'll see what I can do about that.* It was just what they did. "At five, then."

51

Whatever the press knows, or does not know, Dahlia's status as mother of one of the missing soldiers is no secret in the headquarters building of the Israel Police. Only several days earlier she was a resented stranger parachuted into the ranks of a closed and somewhat xenophobic constabulary. Now she has become an object of sympathy, one of their own. The young policewoman who had that first day shown her to an office in the second sub-basement now rises from her reception desk in the lobby as if meeting Dahlia for the first time. "Chief superintendent."

Dahlia pretends not to see the look on the girl's face. "Is Zeltzer in the building?"

"I just want to say—"

"Thank you"—she looks down at the girl's name tag—"Sarit. It's not necessary."

"We all feel—"

"Please call Zeltzer and tell him I'm coming up."

Walking away Dahlia thinks, *What a bitch I must seem. I don't want to be like this. I really don't. But I won't have their pity, as though it's a done deed. As though once the bastards have Ari, they have him and I'll never get him back, never see him under the wedding canopy, never hold those particular grandchildren. What is that,* she thinks in the elevator, *prophylactic bitterness, bitterness before the fact?* The elevator stops. Third floor. A uniformed captain steps in, a face she has never seen.

He pauses. "Going up?"

"All the way."

He gets off on the fifth, then abruptly turns, gives her a thumbs-up.

She finds herself grimacing, then returns the gesture.

In the time it takes to reach the next floor she thinks, *The old Dahlia, the one who is dead, would have chosen a different finger.* Something has turned within her. She knows it. *I will not be my mother,* she thinks. *Not even if the worst happens. But the worst won't happen. I won't let it. Who the hell do they think they're dealing with? This is my son, my firstborn, my Ari. Fuck with my family? Fuck you.*

She finds Zeltzer is in his office with two officers, one in civilian clothes. He puts up his hand as she comes to the door. There is supposed to be a secretary at the desk in the outer office, but Dahlia has never seen her. Or him. Nobody. The desk is neat, in-basket and out-basket equally empty. A stack of papers. A blue sweater on the back of the desk chair, one of those hand-knitted cardigans with a button front. It could be a man's, it could be a woman's. *Probably quit and left the sweater,* she thinks. *Who could stand Zeltzer?*

Her commander waves her in as the two officers leave. They give her the same look.

She offers a weak smile, just the slightest flexing of her lips, an instant and it is gone. "Chief commissioner, we need to talk."

"Clearly. You'd better sit."

She does so. "I had a word with Jumblatt last night."

"I was compelled to leave early. I would have preferred to be here myself to—"

"I would have preferred you stay out of my area of authority."

He selects a cigar from a lacquered wooden box on his desk.

Absurdly, she thinks, *Dudik smokes better ones. There is no money in the civil service.*

He rolls the cigar around in his hand. "You should be happy I haven't suspended you, Advocate Barr. This is not an optimal situation."

"Chief Supt. Barr."

"Correct." He puts the cigar down, a prop, perhaps a crutch. He purses his lips. "Let us be Chaim and Dahlia for a moment. Is that all right?"

"Do you really expect to me to stand aside and let your incompetents fuck this up as they do everything else?" She nearly spits it out: "Chaim."

"Your son is a soldier, Dahlia."

"He's not yet twenty years old."

"The Bedouin, too. Soldiers. For better or worse, it's an Army matter."

"Let me tell you about this Army matter. Ari breast-fed until he was two. He wouldn't separate, glued to it, to me. When he was three, they found a tumor in his leg. After it was cut out I carried him around for a month. All through school he got into trouble for talking back to his teachers. Every week I used to have to go there and smooth it over. Chief commissioner, I don't—"

"Chaim. Please."

"Chaim, I don't give a damn if this is an Army affair. This is a mother's affair. I don't care about anything but my son. Neither you nor the Army will make all the decisions here."

"You understand that there exists a larger question. A political dimension. In the event there is a prisoner exchange, there must not be a mark on Al-Masri. He will lie anyway. That we can't help. But he must not be touched."

"You people, you can't possibly understand."

Again he goes for the cigar. He rolls it between his fingers, taps it on the desk. "I lost mine at eighteen," Zeltzer says. He is half looking away. "He wasn't in the Army six months."

In the ensuing silence both of them hear a phone ringing insistently from down the hall. Five rings, six. Then it stops. After a moment it begins to ring again.

"We're shorthanded," Zeltzer says. "They give us desks and phones, but no one to answer them. For a year I have been trying to change the phone system so that an unanswered call will roll over to a manned desk. It's primitive. There is never any money for the Police."

"I'm so sorry, chief commissioner. I . . ."

"Please. Chaim. My wife . . . you don't want to know. She never got over it. I live with two ghosts. The boy's, and hers. They say for some the hair turns white overnight. Just like that, like paint. With her it didn't happen. Nothing happened. She just . . . died."

"I shouldn't have—"

He waves her off. "It doesn't change anything. It's just the way it is."

"It won't end, will it?" It is as if someone inside her is speaking.

"Not in our lifetime," he says. "Not in our children's, those that survive. My parents brought me from Russia when I was ten. They wanted me to live without hearing *filthy Jew* in the street. They wanted me to grow up free, to be a free Jew in a free Jewish land. But nothing is free, is it? Especially freedom."

"Chaim, I need to handle this."

As though coming to a decision, Zeltzer returns the cigar to its lacquered wooden box. "I'm not the most pleasant commander, am I? My men fear me. They don't love me. You feel the same. Most people do."

"I thought you're a piece of shit."

He laughs, just enough. It comes out as a snort. "I have been called worse. The monsters killed my son. I became like them. Every night I awaken bathed in sweat. It doesn't stop. It will never stop."

"One day it must."

"You'll see, Dahlia. Even if your boy is saved. You won't be. You'll be like me."

"Chaim . . ."

Zeltzer clears his throat, his voice dropping an octave. "Chief Supt. Barr, pursuant to instructions from the political echelon, I officially inform you that I have forbidden the use of extraordinary measures relating to the interrogation of prisoner Mohammed Al-Masri." His voice shrinks to a whisper. "What in fact you do with him is your own business. Dismissed."

52

Three armed men enter the room in which Ari and Salim sleep. Light floods in from the open door. Ari opens one eye, then closes it. They have been in darkness for many hours. Who knows how long? Salim sleeps on, his head in Ari's lap.

"No more for this one," Ari says in stilted Arabic. His eyes adjust. "He will die."

One of the men says, "It is you we require."

Ari does not move.

"Come, rise."

Ari arranges their filthy blanket into a ball, slipping it under Salim's head as he gets to his feet. He is unsteady. Two films run simultaneously through his mind. In one a bad thing is about to happen; in the other he is about to be released. He thinks, *Not the good film. They would be releasing us together.* Then he thinks, *But it could be me. It could be one at a time.* As he puts his hands behind his back for the handcuffs he sees the long drive to the border in the company of Red Cross personnel, men with short-cropped blond hair wearing spectacles and starched, pressed clothes, asking if he wants a cigarette or a candy bar. Swiss chocolate that—

They have arrived at the makeshift television studio.

53

In the hushed room with the garage door–sized electronic map, the eyes of a dozen officers are fixed on the video playing on a large screen. It is all too familiar: the martial music, the yellow and green flag of Hezbollah, the title beneath it— FREE MOHAMMED EDWARD AL-MASRI in English and Arabic—and then the inevitable action whose only sound track is the thwack of broomsticks striking the boy's stomach and then his back, his stomach and then his back, a kind of rhythm section for the boy's cries as they ebb and flow like an oboe solo overlaid against a bass line of thwacks. The rhythm is steady, unaltered, but the boy's cries follow some atonal musical text: He cries out differently from a hit in the stomach or the kidneys, each distinctive wailing note cut short only by the next stroke. Like some dissonant symphony, it seems to go on without form until finally it just stops, at which point the boy is left hanging by his wrists like a beef carcass, silent and raw.

But still alive.

His captors make sure of that. Only alive is he worth anything, and only suffering is he worth a good deal more.

While two of Kobi's specialists begin a frame-by-frame analysis of the footage, which soon enough will be playing in television newsrooms around the world after it is determined how much torture is too much for the general public and how much is necessary to remain competitive in the business of news, Kobi moves to a desk at the far end of the room. Here he is unlikely to be overheard. He dials a number.

"The chief of staff is in a meeting," an adjutant says on the other end.

"Tell him it's a matter of urgency."

In a few moments, Aviv Toledano's rich baritone comes on the line. His hobby is singing. There is in fact a professional singer with close to the same name, one Avi Toledano. The general's critics like to say that the country would be better protected with the singer in charge of the IDF. "Kobi, I was expecting this call."

"Then I don't have to—"

"Just clear it with Chaim Zeltzer."

"You'll pave the way?"

"It's all dream work at this point. Hypothetical."

"If it happens—"

"A deal is a deal, Kobi. I promised, the prime minister gave it his stamp of approval. In a military crisis, you are reactivated at your request. Period."

"I'm in your debt."

"Be that as it may, you're in Zeltzer's employ. Clear it with him."

"Toli . . ."

"The trouble with this country, everyone wants to be a hero."

Kobi does not feel like a hero. It is he who will have to tell Dahlia that the next video stars her son. In a half hour or so he will go to her office. This is not something he wants her to see on CNN.

54

This time she has Al-Masri brought to her office. *There is no sense in extending the charade,* she thinks. *If the man does not already know, then it is time he does.* Besides which, unlike the interview room, her office can be locked from within. The two constables leave.

"You're no longer pretending," Al-Masri says.

"I never did. It was all you." Dahlia pulls a chair opposite. Even she is surprised at her own composure. She thinks: *This must be what it is for an actor. After hours, perhaps days, of stage fright, insecurity, anxiety, he sets foot onstage, and then, poof, it is all gone. There is only the role.* She lights a cigarette. "Do you want one?"

"I don't smoke."

"Are you sure?"

"I don't smoke. I never did."

Dahlia blows a stream of blue smoke in his face. "Actually, I don't remember you smoking. We all smoked in high school. You didn't."

"Please get that out of my face."

She continues blowing smoke. "Tell me about your family, Edward."

He tries to turn away but his torso is locked in place. He can move only his head. "I have nothing to tell you."

"Tell me you wish to return to them."

THE LIE

"You're wasting your time."

"I'll be the judge of that." She pretends to smile. Even the most beautiful woman becomes ugly when that happens, mouth twisting in a grimace, eyes dead. She exhales smoke again. "And jury." She gets up, goes to the door, and locks it.

Outside, hearing the tumblers fall into place, the two constables exchange a look.

"Let me just explain this to you in a way you can understand. Zero subtlety. Of course as you know there is no word in Hebrew for *subtlety*. It's not a Jewish concept." She blows a stream of smoke in his eyes. "In a moment I will prove that you do smoke."

"I demand to see a lawyer. And the Canadian ambassador."

"There is a quaint American expression that I learned from a dear friend: *And people in hell want ice water.* Edward, you are in hell. You just don't know it. And you will smoke."

He turns his head away.

She pulls a scarf from her purse, knots it, gags him. It is a curiously intimate act, like helping a child into his coat, or not driving through a crosswalk when a pedestrian is approaching the corner but is not yet there. "Edward . . . I don't mind calling you Edward. You may call me chief superintendent. Many believe otherwise, but in life we do get to choose what we will be. Though some of us make better choices than others."

He tries to say something. It comes out muffled, noise.

"Now, Edward, it may seem counterproductive that I must silence you to make you talk. But I'd rather not alarm the constables. They're just simple cops. Me, I'm . . . not so simple." Slowly, almost erotically, she unbuttons his shirt. "Did you say you didn't smoke? Let us see." She holds the lit end of her cigarette to his chest.

His scream is merely a soft noise. He shakes his head back and forth.

"Well, well. Edward, it turns out you do smoke after all. Where there is fire, there is smoke, no?" She pauses. "What, cat got your tongue? I love those American expressions. Do you have them in Canada? No? Yes? Would you like to say something, Professor Al-Masri?" She tousles his hair. "Shall we perform our little exercise again? Yes? No? Perhaps just once more?"

She grinds the cigarette out on his chest as he writhes, screaming silently, tossing his head uncontrollably. "All right, then. We've demonstrated that with the application of fire, Edward Al-Masri, who doesn't smoke, does indeed. Now, Edward, I'm going to remove the gag. When I do, you will remain perfectly silent. Should you make one noise, even a cough, I will gag you again. I have a full pack of cigarettes in my purse. Do I make myself clear? Yes? No?"

He nods vigorously.

She removes the gag. "Remember, not a sound unless I ask you a direct question. Do you understand?"

"Yes."

"Now, Edward, pay attention. I'm only an amateur at this, so you'll have to be patient. Just answer the questions. They're not difficult. Yes?"

"Yes."

"What is your full name?"

"Edward Al-Masri. You know this."

"Your *full* name."

"Edward Mohammed Al-Masri."

"Of which countries are you a citizen?"

"I am a citizen of Canada."

"No other country?"

"I told you. I renounce my Israeli citizenship. As a Canadian citizen, I demand—"

She lights another cigarette. "This is not CNN, Edward. Nor

148

am I one of your impressionable students at McGill University. How old are you?"

"Forty-four."

"Indeed you are. Soon to be forty-five. Not the best age for a woman, but for a man still very nice. Now, tell me about your wife and child."

He stares at the cigarette. "Genevieve."

"Age?"

"Thirty-six."

"Son?"

"Edward Jr. Twenty months."

"Good. Now tell me, Edward, do you wish to see your wife and son again?"

"I do."

"And is it truly your belief that by not cooperating you will make that happen?"

"Look, Dahlia, I know precisely what you can and cannot do. The law is clear. If you burn me, I will inform the court. Torture is not permitted. You know that."

"Oh, Edward." She stuffs the gag back in, takes the cigarette, and as she speaks burns him slowly in three places, ignoring his reaction as he twists in the wheelchair. "If only you knew how little I like not to be taken seriously. In the courtroom it galled me when a judge did not take me seriously. When I was a young officer in the Army it drove me crazy not to be taken seriously by the men around me. If I were honest with myself, I'd have to say my marriage began to collapse the moment my husband failed to take me seriously. In fact, I chose a lover who takes me very seriously. For you not to take me seriously, a man in your position—"

She is interrupted by a loud knocking at the door.

"Dahlia. It's Kobi. Please unlock the door."

"I need to know one thing, Edward. I need to know who precisely is behind this little operation, who it is that is holding my son. And I need to know how to find him. Now I'm going to remove your gag again. We really don't have much time." She goes to the desk and removes the service pistol from her purse.

"Dahlia! Open the fucking door!"

"All this romantic business of cigarettes and conversation, it's a luxury now, isn't it?" She cocks the pistol and holds it to his head, with the other hand removing the gag.

"Open the door or I'll break it down!"

"On the count of three, you will give me what I require, or you will die. One . . ."

The door is being battered.

"Two . . ."

The door is about to give way.

"Good-bye, Edward."

"Tawfeek Nur-al-Din! Somewhere in Beirut!"

The doorpost splinters as the door flies open.

"Dahlia, put down the gun."

"Certainly," she says.

55

Their usual place in Tel Aviv is an always crowded café overlooking the harbor in Jaffa, from which Arab port in 1909 a dozen families moved down the beach to found Israel's first Jewish city. Eventually the tiny Jewish settlement grew to envelop and annex the Arab port: Tel Aviv–Jaffa is the city's official name, though no one ever calls it that except before mayoral elections, when candidates show up in Jaffa to promise improved garbage collection and more traffic lights.

The television above the bar is showing Arab demonstrations in another Arab town, Israel's largest: "Meanwhile, here in Umm al-Fahm, rioting continues as demonstrators clash with police." On the screen several hundred Israeli Arabs hold signs in Hebrew and English that read FULL RIGHTS FOR ARAB CITIZENS! and ALL PALESTINIANS ARE BROTHERS! And WHERE IS PROF AL-MASRI? A phalanx of Border Police in riot gear holds them back.

"You know I don't have any political opinions," Floyd tells Dahlia as the newscast continues. Around them, waiters step deftly between tables full of couples watching the sunset over the small harbor that was the gateway to the Holy Land before modern Jewish ports were built at Haifa to the north, Ashdod to the south, and at Eilat on the Red Sea.

"Not having political opinions is itself a political opinion," Dahlia says with easy derision. "We've gone over this."

"I'm neutral because I have to be."

"Is that why you came to Tel Aviv this evening? To tell me you don't have—what is it you like to say?—a dog in this fight?"

"I miss you."

"I'm here."

"You don't have to make it harder than it already is."

"There are some word plays that are no longer amusing. Floyd, what do you have for me?"

"A colleague of mine at CNN owes your lover a favor."

"I'm listening."

"Our guy in Beirut. He's picked up something. Maybe nothing."

Dahlia listens hard, but controls her face the way she would in court, where a good defense attorney must never show emotion. "Okay."

"An address."

For a moment she thinks the boys' names have been announced. Or leaked. *No*, she thinks, *I would have been told. It would be on the radio. It would be on the same television set in this very restaurant.* It is settled government policy: No release of the names of hostages until absolutely necessary, lest the enemy find a way to use this information—either directly, in order to break the hostages with "information" about their parents' suffering, or indirectly, in the form of heightened pressure on the government once the press begins to incite public opinion for a speedy resolution. There is as well the stated purpose: protecting the families. "An address for what?"

"It's from someone in, let's call it, a position to know. It could be nothing. I figure, now that you're with the police, it might be useful."

She thinks: *Absolutely he doesn't know.* "Floyd, please don't draw this out."

"I thought you like it when I do."

"Floyd, please. Be an adult."

He passes a folded paper across the narrow table.

She reads it, puts it in her purse. "Is that it? An address?"

A waiter comes by, an Arab. "Another drink?" A glance at their faces, and he leaves.

"You won't say where you got it, right?"

"I won't say."

"My colleague has a pal in the Lebanese security services. Not exactly a friend of Hezbollah. A Christian."

"Yes?"

"It may be where the hostages are held."

Dahlia rises. "I've got to go."

"No guarantees. It's something, that's all."

"I understand." Softening, she bends to kiss his cheek. "And I'm grateful."

"Just don't mention . . ."

"No one will know."

"It's my career, that's all."

"Thanks."

"If anything does go down, I'd appreciate . . ."

"I know. It's your career."

He watches her fly down the stone stairs to the waiting white Subaru. It takes off, siren screaming, lights ablaze. He signals the waiter. "I'll have another."

56

OFFICE OF THE PRIME MINISTER
Security Cabinet

Memorandum of Record

Present

The PRIME MINISTER, presiding
AL-SHEIKH, Yarden, Minister of Internal Security
BLUMENTHAL, Shai, Minister of Defense
ADMONI, David, Minister Without Portfolio
ARAD, Zalman, Security Adviser to the PM
ROSCH, Dror, Cabinet Secretary

Absent

BEN-DOV, Carmela, Foreign Minister

The Prime Minister

We'll make this brief. The Foreign Minister is abroad. For the record, Carmela has delegated her vote to myself. Time is short. David, your report?

David Admoni, Minister Without Portfolio

Pursuant to instructions from the PM, I have been tasked with responsibility regarding the missing soldiers, Barr and Ibn-Aziz. Having consulted with the key officials, all present, I report the following: [a]

THE LIE

The two boys are in dire circumstance, their captors using torture and circulating videos of same to the media and on the Internet in a clear attempt to influence public opinion within Israel; [b] From a variety of sources, we have identified the responsible official within Hezbollah and a possible location for the prisoners within Beirut; [c] Our analysts have put the likelihood of the location being accurate at sixty to seventy-five percent, with the caveat that the boys may be moved at any time; [d] A team has been readied for a rescue operation and is standing by; [e] Lastly, it has been confirmed that Hezbollah is willing to trade their prisoners for one Mohammed Al-Masri, who is being held in Police custody—it has been communicated that the cousins wish to make a propaganda statement to the effect that it is no longer true that one Israeli prisoner is worth thousands of Arab terror prisoners but that the tables are now turned: One Arab prisoner is worth multiple Israelis.

The Prime Minister
For this they are torturing our young men? To boast?

Yarden Al-Sheikh, Minister of Internal Security
Clearly, there is an internal aspect. It is certain any such trade would give encouragement to Israeli Arabs in their current series of demonstrations, whose timing is—we need not speculate—suspicious. It is my belief that the cousins are attempting to open up a second front within Israel proper. Once this genie is out of the bottle . . .

The Prime Minister
Unfortunately, I'm afraid Washington is, as usual, cautioning restraint. The Foreign Minister is there now. As I am certain you are aware, we are looking at an arms deal that could very well transform

the IDF, particularly the Air Force, into an entity whose range is virtually limitless.

Shai Blumenthal, Minister of Defense
With all due respect, that is a consideration that should be left to another time. The national defense takes precedence, but no defense decision should be made with a gun held to our head. It is the policy of this nation to rescue any and all soldiers held behind enemy lines when we have adequate resources to effect such a rescue and sufficient certainty of their location. If we could go to Entebbe in the middle of Africa, we can go to Beirut. We have been there before.

Yarden Al-Sheikh, Minister of Internal Security
It can hardly hurt if we bring back a Muslim soldier of the IDF. Let them then demonstrate that in Israel Arabs are second-class citizens.

The Prime Minister
Negative implications? Zalman?

Zalman Arad, Security Adviser to the PM
The same as always. Heavy losses. Failure. The first is the price, the second merely a risk factor, which we have determined is reasonable. The Americans will be angry. This is not an issue. We are talking about two of our best young men, who are suffering torture and may lose their lives in the process. We must come to a speedy decision.

The Prime Minister
As usual, Zalman, we are grateful for your perspective. Those who would vote against an emergency rescue mission, please raise your hand. Otherwise let the record show unanimity, and let us pray for a positive outcome.

57

In the sixth-floor conference room adjacent to Zeltzer's office, the chief commissioner has not bothered to unwrap his cigar. He simply fingers it, then sticks it back in his chest pocket. "We'll not draw this out. You might as well tell her."

Kobi turns to Dahlia. "I'm back in the Army. Temporarily."

"Seventy-two hours," Zeltzer says.

"It's all I need."

"Finally, I get an intelligence chief who doesn't need to remove his boots to count to twenty, and the Army takes him back. In seventy-two hours you could be killed."

"Intelligence officers don't get killed. We're too intelligent."

"I don't understand," Dahlia says.

"We're going in," Kobi says. "Bit of a secret."

"The address is good?"

"Maybe. There is activity in that spot. But they move hostages constantly. With so many informers all around, it's their first line of defense. Still, a television studio is not so easy to move and set up again and again. We have some degree of confidence." He pauses. "But little time." He picks up the remote control. "Dahlia, it's been decided you shouldn't have to see this first on CNN."

Dahlia stands in horror. Ari's face is not shown on the screen. But a mother knows her own son.

157

Zeltzer rises quickly to hold her. "It'll be all right. They're professionals. They'll get them out."

She collapses into his arms, weeping silently. Suddenly she stops. "Uri, Dudik. I can't be here."

"Zaid," Zeltzer says.

The Druze takes her arm. "Come, Dahlia. I'll ride with you."

When they leave, the two men face each other.

Zeltzer says, "They'll beat the boy until there's nothing left. They'll stretch it out."

"That's why it's called terrorism. It's not aimed at Dahlia's kid or the Bedouin. It's aimed at us."

"More beatings like that," Zeltzer says, "the boys are finished."

58

At a large military base in northern Israel, preparations are well under way for a mission whose code name is Heavy Smoker. Its existence is known only to about five hundred IDF personnel. However, in Israel military secrets are said to be relative: Not only the officers and soldiers directly involved know what is going on, but all their relatives. The specifics may be veiled, but that something *is* going on can hardly remain a secret to thousands of wives and husbands, parents and children. To call Heavy Smoker a secret is to refer only to the details, the how and when, not the what.

What does the crew know who are spraying matte-black paint on two Yasur-class helicopters—upgraded American Chinooks—other than that they will soon be put to use? Why soon? Forget that the crew was called up on emergency orders. Forget that the brass personally inspects every aspect of their work. Forget that the paint they are using has an intended life expectancy of just days before it peels off by itself in the sun and rain. The crew is told nothing, but one need not be privy to operations planning to know that two IDF soldiers are being held hostage in Lebanon and that they will die if left to the whims of their sadistic captors.

What do the artists know who are carefully inscribing in Arabic and French the proper identifying marks onto a gray 1978

Cadillac ambulance, or those who are preparing four white BMW motorcycles with the markings of Le Police Nationale du Liban? Told nothing, they know enough.

The same is true for the seven master tailors working from designs prepared by professional pattern makers, all pressed into service from the Israeli fashion industry. What need they be told other than that they must quickly create the following costumes: twenty extremely elegant Italian army uniforms, authentic down to the buttons, nine short-trousered Ugandan army uniforms, four uniforms of the motorcycle corps of the Lebanese *gendarmie*, replete with somewhat worn black leather jackets? Meanwhile, two custom shoemakers in an adjoining room are tasked with creating complementary knee-high boots, and across the hall costumers from Habima, the national theater, put the finishing touches on theatrically authentic helmets to complete the charade. Already accounted for are dozens of shabby costumes suitable to Lebanese laborers, two cocktail dresses with deep décolletage, two fur stoles, two pairs of gold-colored five-inch heels, sufficient paste jewelry for ten Israeli bridesmaids, two tuxedos with appropriately ruffled shirts, bow ties, cummerbunds and patent-leather shoes, a nice selection of white medical attire, and one dark gray chauffeur's uniform replete with a peaked cap that was used only the month before in an Israel Television comedy about a simple farming family that wins the lottery and hires a chauffeur to drive their tractor.

Have these tailors, shoemakers, costumers, and—in yet another building—makeup artists been informed about what is planned for their creations? Absolutely not. Do they know that nearby in what had been—before the British decamped in 1948—a mess hall for His Majesty's Fourth Mechanized Grenadiers, some eighty members of the most elite units, the ablest commandos in the IDF, are even now about to be addressed by their chief of staff? Certainly not. Are they aware that every stitch, every placket, every detail will shortly be employed in a plan so audacious none of its operational details will be made public in their lifetimes? Without a doubt. Like every other citizen of Israel, they have watched the lurid videos on Israel Television, read the newspapers, talked about what must be done over Elite Turkish coffee or HaTzvi arak or Goldstar beer. And all of them have answered their spouses' questions about why they have disappeared with a raised eyebrow and a wink, and said nothing. And in saying nothing said it all.

59

Now, in the former mess that has become a military lecture hall, the eighty IDF personnel, all men except for two women, stand as the chief of staff strides in, followed closely by one Col. Gadi of the well-known lisp and one Medical Officer Itzik, bespectacled, short and chubby, the country's leading expert on battle trauma—the IDF censor forbids identification of most serving personnel by anything other than first name, though every Israeli and his parakeet knows who they are. A few steps behind, one Col. Kobi enters the hall wearing a uniform he thought he might never don again.

The chief of staff—who in meetings at the political level, such as the Security Cabinet, might appear restrained and reserved, even diffident—is now in his element. "As you were," he says with such authority that everyone in the room is abruptly off their feet as though one long string has pulled them all back down to their seats. "I'm here not to interfere with what I believe to be a well-planned operation but to wish you a successful mission and a safe return. In case you are unaware of the significance of this operation, understand the following: [a] We have a single tactical objective—the safe return of two of our boys—but beyond that a strategic goal, which is to destroy the enemy's use of kidnapping to impair morale within Israel and to split the population. The enemy wishes us to face two alternatives: Negotiate for the hostages, *any* hostages, or see them suffer and die. We offer a third choice: Take the hostages back and wipe out the kidnappers; [b] This operation will transpire in a civilian setting. Pro forma, the enemy is hiding among the innocent. As always, we will do what is possible to spare civilian lives; [c] Our boys are suffering grave punishments. If indeed all we can do is bring back their bodies, that is what we will do. If that is clear, in the name of the nation I wish you the blessing of the just."

All stand to return his salute. In an instant he exits as briskly as he entered.

Col. Gadi takes the podium. "Settle down, gentlemen," he says with his mild lisp. He looks over his troops. "And ladies. We will review operational details once more, following a briefing by Dr. Itzik and Res. Col. Kobi, who has been reactivated to serve as mission intelligence officer. Kobi?"

"Except for the chow," Kobi says, "it's good to be back. My friends, here is what we know." He picks up a pointer. "And what we don't."

60

At precisely the same time, in his apartment in Beirut, Tawfeek Nur-al-Din, writing in a fine Arabic hand, completes a letter to his wife in Athens. As is common with many high-level Palestinian commanders, Tawfeek's family is tucked safely away in Europe so that Israeli agents cannot take them as counter-hostages. The envelope is addressed to a flat in Paris that is little more than a drop box. Upon receipt, it will be forwarded to a second address in Barcelona and from there sent on to a post office in Athens, where it will be picked up by a courier who will then deliver it to a Palestinian-owned café off Independence Square. Once a week Fatima Nur-al-Din stops there for coffee and baklava, and ice cream for the children, a boy of six and a girl of four.

This elaborate system, the coordinates of which are changed regularly, is meant to put Israeli intelligence off the scent. They are, in the main, unnecessary. Despite its fearsome—and often undeserved—reputation for merciless efficiency, the Mossad and associated minor agencies are perennially underfunded and consequently understaffed. Unless there is a chance that Commander Tawfeek himself is expected to visit his family, there is little reason to surveil his family beyond monitoring his wife's telephone conversations. And one significant reason not to: By custom, if not outright protocol, the wives and children of enemy operatives are specifically exempt from what is called "administrative interference." Even the wife of the late Yassir Arafat was effectively immune during the years she lived openly in an opulent suite at the Bristol Hotel in Paris.

But paranoia is a constant companion of Arab terrorists, who project upon their enemies in the West their own lack of scruples regarding non-combatants. This is not to say Israel will stay operations against specific targets when there is danger to their families—otherwise, terrorists would know they are pro-tected in their homes—but Israel has not descended to specifi-cally targeting the innocent.

Oh, my dearest, Commander Tawfeek's letter concludes, *once again the necessary precludes the pleasurable. Some day, when we have regained the homeland and driven the savages into the sea, you and I and the children will walk on the beach and dip our toes in the water of freedom. Please do not fear. I have taken every precau-tion. The Small Satan is now in delicate military negotiations with the Grand Satan and dares not offend its master with an attack on a neighboring country. In time the exchange will indeed take place. Thus encouraged, all true Muslims will join with us to reclaim our homeland and resume the illustrious history that has been interrupted for a thousand years. Embrace the children in my name, and remind them of their father who loves them. With desire, your Tawfeek.*

61

At 1:40 that morning, a moonlit night that no one would have chosen for such a mission, the two matte-black Yasurs fly low over the Mediterranean, skimming the whitecaps, six missile-armed Super Apaches flying shotgun ahead and above. No lights, radio silence.

To the northeast, the streets of central Beirut are still lit up; its cafés and discos will be doing business until dawn. From this distance, the pulsing center of the Arab world's ultimate party town reveals itself in the blurry white lines of automobile head-lights. Secondary concentrations of light indicate casinos in the hills overlooking Beirut and a half-dozen nightclubs north of the city. In contrast to these hot spots, the windows of the Leb-anese capital's three- and four-story apartment buildings glow softly with the shimmer of big-screen televisions, the Western-ized equivalent of the Bedouin fire pit, around which families are still gathered at close to two in the morning. Beirutis stay up late.

This does not make the mission any easier. According to real-time intelligence compiled through satellite surveillance capable of identifying the brand on a cigarette pack, Hezbol-lah fighters are heavily dug in on the border between Chris-tian East and Muslim West Beirut. They control all four traffic arteries leading inland from the sea. If the two IDF soldiers are indeed being held in West Beirut, getting there will require a three-mile journey across an insomniac city cut into jittery segments by paranoid militias. And this is merely the entry ticket: Around the target site, an unknown number of defenders are established in a strong perimeter, including control of the rooftops. Until engagement, any contact with locals, both Hezbollah and civilian—the latter of which can be trusted to sound an alarm: it pays well—must be limited to French for those wearing Italian uniforms, English for the Ugandans, and for all others Lebanese-inflected Arabic. From takeoff until the unit fires its first shot, not one word of Hebrew will be spoken.

To the Air Force officers piloting the Yasurs, this hardly matters. Their single-minded objective is to land their eighty-nine-foot craft within hundred-foot-diameter landing zones among the dunes southwest of the city. The landing zones are to be lit with flares at precisely 2:11 A.M. This is to be handled by a pre-insertion force of six who arrived that evening on commercial flights from Paris, Rome, and Athens. The six carry passports from Egypt, France, Greece, Germany (two), and Turkey. Precisely at 2:11, the pilots spot two impossibly tiny triangles of light.

Yasur One peels off, followed by Yasur Two, shadowed by four Super Apaches hovering at one hundred feet in order to deal with unexpected resistance. The remaining pair of attack helicopters remain in tactical reserve at eight hundred feet.

Even before Yasur One touches ground, its rear gate swings down to form a ramp as commandos leap off to take up protective positions until the four police motorcycles within roll off safely onto the sand. Fifteen seconds later, Yasur Two touches down, its own ramp disgorging six commandos dressed as Arab laborers and four in more exotic dress—two male officers in tuxedos, one of whom speaks with a mild lisp, and two elegantly attired women in cocktail dresses and elaborate wigs, one blonde, one redhead: Nurit and Alexandra, both Russian-speaking children of emigrants from the former Soviet Union. They are members of a Mossad special operations unit based in the Persian Gulf watering hole of Dubai, where Russian beauties are in high demand. The two wear flats, but their large gaudily sequined purses contain five-inch heels, to say nothing of the Uzi machine pistols that can take down three dozen men in one burst. Last to exit is the meticulously authentic pearl-gray 1978 Cadillac ambulance marked with the Red Crescent. Augmented with four-wheel drive and other nonstandard equipment, it holds Dr. Itzik and four men in white medical uniforms, whose military specialties concern the saving of some lives and the taking of others.

Waiting for the force's arrival on the dirt road that parallels the beach are a new Mercedes limousine, three taxis, a refrigerated seafood van, a glazier's pickup truck carrying four-by-eight-foot mirror panels vertically on its sides, a garbage truck, and a white American-made school bus with black UN markings. All of these have been "borrowed" for the occasion by Israeli operatives permanently resident in Beirut, not all of them Israelis. Considering the expense of maintaining operatives in an enemy country, replete with convincing cover stories, employing locals becomes not only cheap but efficient: Locals know where to liberate a garbage truck or a limo or a seafood van. A good many of these operatives are Christians with a standing grudge against Hezbollah for its ongoing Islamization of what was, until recently, Christian-dominated Lebanon. All were trained at a special camp for foreign assets at a discreet facility in southern Israel.

In a matter of seconds the vehicles scatter, the two Yasurs lifting off to join the Apaches as they move out over the Med. Other than the tracks of the ambulance and motorcycles and the footprints of the unit sprinting to the road above it, no sign is left on the beach of the invasion force. In a matter of half an hour this evidence too will be erased by the incoming tide.

As the helicopters disappear, three Super Dvora Mk III patrol boats take up positions offshore. These carry sufficient sea-to-ground missiles to provide a meaningful distraction should the rescue force require it. Just over the border, thirty-two miles to the south, a flight of fourteen drones is launched, four outfitted with live television cameras. The remaining eight are what their Israel Air Force controllers call Killer Smurfs, flying bombs set to detonate on impact. At a base one mile south of the border, a brigade of helicopter-borne paratroopers stands by in case things go very wrong.

Each unit of the team moving toward Beirut travels alone, each on a separate route. Each must penetrate, circumnavigate, or neutralize the perilous, sometimes fatal Lebanese equivalent of traffic lights, the roadblock.

62

In Caesarea, Dudik and Uri sleep together propped on a couch, the father holding his seventeen-year-old son as if he were a small child. Both are exhausted from crying.

Damn CNN, Dahlia thinks. *Damn the wonders of technology.*

She sits on the other side of the sliding glass doors smoking by the edge of the pool, her feet dangling in the dark water. The air is cool, as cool as she had been when they watched the new video, her own child being tortured there on the television in their living room. Of course she had seen it before, the complete version, before CNN edited out the worst. Still, she would have thought it would affect her again the same way or worse. But no, it was almost comforting that her son is still alive. *Imagine that,* she thinks, *I have watched my son being tortured and managed not to cry. Maybe Dudik is right to call me cold. Maybe Floyd is right to call me a bitch. Maybe Zalman Arad is right to have chosen me for a job whose very parameters require a kind of cranial disconnectedness.* She had always thought of herself as warm, passionate, caring. Now she sees the other side, the side others see. *So what?* she thinks. *So what if I have become this way or always was and maybe always will be. It's a tough neighborhood. You have to be as tough, if not tougher. You have a husband, even if he is a soon-to-be-divorced husband, and a son. You have to lead by example. The bastards want you to be weak, to be broken by grief. I will not be broken by grief. They will get him out. And if they don't? Don't think of that. One step at a time. If Kobi spoke of seventy-two hours, then even now something is being done to save Ari, to save both boys. The Bedouin kid's mother did not show fear. She showed anger. Be like her. In seventy-two hours it will be done, one way or another.*

Uri had thrown up. Right there in the living room, Dudik holding his head as he used to over the toilet bowl when Uri was a child with a stomach flu. It was Dudik who had comforted him afterward until both had fallen asleep, worn out by their tears. All she had been able to do was walk out onto the patio, sitting silent by the edge of the pool.

She stubs out her cigarette in a glass ashtray etched with the logo of Château Fuente, a memento Dudik had not bothered to take with his other belongings. Abruptly, out of nowhere, she thinks, *If not for Uri I would swim nude. When is the last time I swam nude?*

She looks behind her. The boy is sound asleep. She thinks then of Dudik. *What if Dudik wakes and finds me that way?* Only days ago she would have considered it something a divorcing woman must not do. How odd that now she feels a closeness to Dudik that she has not felt in years.

She slips out of her shift and eases her way into the still water, its temperature not that much different from her own. It is as if she has become one with the water, and for the first time in days finds herself relaxing, her breasts bobbing free as she floats on her back. In a moment, for the first time in days, she is deeply asleep, buoyed by her breasts, and by hope.

63

Flanked by four Lebanese Police motorcycles, two fore and two aft, the white school bus marked *UN* on all sides and on the roof, a common troop carrier for the ubiquitous UNIFIL peacekeeping forces stationed in Lebanon, pulls up before a roadblock on the main east-west road. The barrier forms a choke point between the apartment blocks on either side, from whose windows armed Hezbollah fighters stare down. On either side, an embankment of old cigarette butts lines the street like dirty snow fallen from above. The roadblock is brightly lit. Wrecked cars narrow the wide street so that only one vehicle can pass. From out of one of these, as if from a proper office with a desk and a telephone and a photo of the Hezbollah leader, a thin officer steps.

On the lead motorcycle Kobi knows the man is an officer because he carries in his right hand a distinctive Heckler & Koch VP70 machine pistol. An ungainly affair, it appears to be a handgun to which someone clumsily attached the stock of a rifle on one end and an obscenely long magazine carrying one hundred eighteen 9mm rounds on the other. This is arguably the world's most deadly handgun. Capable of firing twenty-two hundred rounds per minute, it sounds in operation like a chain saw on steroids. Only selected Hezbollah commanders are issued this gun, a mark of status. Armed with their commonplace Kalashnikov automatic rifles, the officer's troopers stand leaning half asleep against the apartment house walls on either side. Thanks to decades of Communist Bloc arms dealing, the Kalashnikov AK-47 is standard issue for every Arab soldier, bodyguard, and terrorist in what security professionals call the ABC, the unstable triangle that stretches from Afghanistan in Central Asia to Beirut in the Middle East to Chad in West Africa. Whether originating in Russia or Romania or China, the AK-47 is the personal weapon of choice wherever Allah is praised.

The officer pointedly ignores the Lebanese motorcycle cops and climbs aboard the bus, which as is normal in Beirut travels with its doors open to catch the Mediterranean breeze. Everyone aboard but the Italian driver is asleep, Africans on one side, Italians on the other. Climbing down, the officer gestures behind him with his machine pistol. "From where are the monkeys?"

"Africa," Kobi says.

"But where in Africa? This interests me."

"Who knows? They are UNIFIL. By the prophet, my dear friend, it is fucking late."

"You don't know from where? Clearly, the white ones are Italian. From the uniforms. Each one must have his own personal tailor."

Kobi turns to the second motorcycle cop, whose name is Yossi. "Achmed, from which country are the black ones?"

"Uganda."

As if the Hezbollah officer requires a translation, Kobi says it again, louder. "He says Uganda."

"Is that a Muslim land?"

"Who knows?"

"If they are Muslim," the Hezbollah officer says, "they should wear long pants. Lebanon is a civilized nation, not the jungle." He waves the bus through.

64

At a second roadblock half a mile to the north, the Mercedes limo is stopped at a makeshift barrier staffed by two young Hezbollah militiamen wearing uniform shirts over jeans and Nike running shoes. They admire the car. Mercedes Benz automobiles are common enough in Lebanon, but a Mercedes limousine is rare. Of course, anything the least bit out of the ordinary would be enough to rouse their interest in the middle of yet another trafficless night.

"Maternal cunt," its chauffeur says in the best street Arabic. "Let me deliver these stinking foreigners to their hotel so I can get some sleep."

Unable to peer through the mirror glass of the windows, one of the Hezbollah men opens the left rear door: Four reprobates, living cartoons, each of the men holding a bottle, the redhead passed out, the blonde in sunglasses grinning back at them, stinking drunk. She says something in Russian, slurred. In a typically ambivalent Arab gesture revealing simultaneous disgust and envy, the militiaman spits on the limousine's windshield and then offers a thumbs-up. Pointing with his Kalashnikov, he waves them through.

65

Not half a kilometer from the second roadblock, a sandbagged machine-gun position faces the entering street, where the seafood van is lined up in front of the glazier's pickup. Without so much as a comment, much less permission, Hezbollah fighters open the van and begin unloading trays of shrimp. The van driver leaps out. "By God, take a bit for your honors, who work in the cold night. But I have a family. Leave me something to sell."

Behind the van, the glazier hits his horn. Taking an interest, a second Hezbollah officer strolls over.

"*Habibi*, for the sake of justice!" the pickup driver says. "From the port in Tripoli I have had the joy of six roadblocks. Please, if you wish to do business with a fish seller, be my guest, but let pass an honest glazier."

The Hezbollah officer smiles in sympathy. He makes the universally understood Middle Eastern sign for patience, thumb and forefinger touching as his hand bobs slowly up and down, then leisurely circles the pickup for a cursory inspection before returning to the glazier. "Why must Muslims be so vain as to need such large mirrors? Do they not know that to make a human image is forbidden?"

"This is not making an image," the glazier says. "These are mirrors. The image makes itself."

The officer laughs, revealing a good-natured understanding of the complications of applying sacred law to a still-profane world. "So late at night for the splitting of theological hairs," he says with a smile. "Please accept my apology." To better make his point, he swings the butt of his Kalashnikov in a wide arc. Secured to the side of the van, the huge mirror shatters in place. "But next time, kindly be more patient. Just as you have a job to do, so too we." He waves the glazier through. The seafood vendor gives up arguing, re-enters his now half-empty van, and— the tax having been paid—follows.

66

The garbage truck with two laborers hanging off the back pulls up before a fourth roadblock narrowed by fifty-gallon oil drums burning scrap wood, Hezbollah fighters warming their hands in the glow. In an instant the garbagemen are off the truck and warming themselves as well. It gets cold hanging off the back of a vehicle going fifty miles an hour in fifty-degree temperature.

Coming up quickly, the Red Crescent ambulance, siren bleating, brakes hard, almost hitting the garbage truck.

The ambulance driver jumps out. He is a sharpshooter named Moshe whose family, originally from Syria, speaks Arabic at home. The accents of Lebanon and western Syria are indistinguishable. "Move this stinking pile! A man is dying of heart failure, and you are blocking the way with offal?"

A Hezbollah officer leaves the warmth of the fires and approaches the ambulance. "Let me see this dying man." He peers into the ambulance. "There is no patient here, dying or otherwise."

"Not here!" the ambulance driver shouts. "There! In the hills. We go to his aid, then to bring him to hospital—unless again we are stopped. Do you wish that poor man's life on your head?!"

The officer sprints to the garbage truck and grabs its driver by his collar through the open window. "Idiot, selfish fool! Move your rolling trash heap. Get going!"

The garbage truck grinds out of the way, leaving room for the ambulance to pass, its siren echoing as it speeds across the sleeping city to join the other units closing on the target site.

67

Minutes later, as the four units converge, Staff Sgt. Ruhama, a nineteen-year-old Israel Air Force remote-flight technician, takes her seat in a control room carved into a cave in the limestone cliffs overlooking the sea at Rosh HaNikra, virtually on the Lebanese border. Like everyone around her, she wears a sweater. The heavy computing power at her fingertips demands the room be kept uncomfortably cold. It is beyond air-conditioned. Meat will not spoil here.

Having grown up with video games, Ruhama is the Israel Air Force's ranking ace when it comes to directing drones in battle. Operating an LED panel over which is an array of fourteen live-action monitors—rigorous testing found that for one controller fourteen drones is optimal: One more and operational efficiency drops by twelve percent—Ruhama settles in and begins the drill she knows so well. She had been out dancing in the nearby beach town of Nahariya until midnight. It is now 2:44 A.M. She remains fresh, energized. Youth has certain advantages.

Behind her stands her unit commander, Maj. David, the son of American ascendants to Israel (one ascends to the Holy Land; one does not simply emigrate). Twenty years earlier his parents pulled him out of a school for the gifted in San Francisco to live in a tiny settlement in Judea, which the world news media calls the West Bank. A lonely child in an unchallenging school, young David soon developed an interest in remote-controlled model planes, building and flying them from the barren hillsides overlooking the hostile Arab villages surrounding the settlement. Over time he attached a tiny television camera to the belly of a two-foot-long aircraft and brought it to the settlement's security chief with the suggestion that the cobbled-together device might provide early warning in case of a terrorist attack. From this adolescent curiosity came Israel's world leadership in drone weaponry.

Maj. David unwraps another stick of gum as he holds to his ear a blue phone with an open line to IAF headquarters one hundred feet underground at the Kiryah in Tel Aviv.

Sgt. Ruhama goes through her checklist. "Airspeed: a hundred and five kilometers per hour. Time to target: four minutes, thirty seconds. Air-to-air visibility: forty-five kilometers. Air-to-ground visibility: category one. All systems in order."

"Arm weapons."

"Units one through ten arming." She takes a sip from one of the six cans of Diet Coke she will drink over her ten-hour shift. "All weapons armed."

"Okay, sergeant. Do your stuff."

"Roger that, David. Doing my stuff."

Her commander unwraps another stick of gum.

68

Over southwestern Beirut eight Killer Smurfs peel off, leaving in reserve two similar explosive-laden aircraft, while four observer drones armed only with extremely high-definition night-vision video cameras circle at fifteen hundred feet, just below cloud cover but well beyond the range of rifle fire from Hezbollah riflemen perched on the rooftops surrounding the target site.

From behind their sandbags, the riflemen look up as the sound of what could only be giant mosquitoes becomes evident, then louder.

Then louder still.

Then fatal.

69

A few blocks away, all four units, engines running, stand by in staging positions. Their radios are silent. There is no need for communication. The signal to move in will be the sound of the first explosion as the drones find their targets.

Before the second explosion all vehicles and personnel are on the move. Whether or not the drones will have destroyed all six Hezbollah positions on the rooftops of the buildings surrounding the target site, the action has commenced. There is no turning back.

70

In her cold room at Rosh Hanikra, Staff Sgt. Ruhama watches on live television as her drones do their work. "Smurfs one through eight on target," she says in the affectless voice of a video gamer with nothing to prove. "Nine and ten standing by." She zooms the images on her television screens. "Number four marginal hit. Looks like a wind gust." In the narrow canyons created by the buildings lining the street a sudden gust can knock the tiny aircraft off target by as much as ten feet. "Taking care of that, commander." With a flick of her joystick, she detaches drone number nine.

71

As the vehicles converge from both ends of the street the rescue force sprints to its objectives. They could do this blindfolded, and in fact have twice among the forty clocked drills they have carried out in a simulation of the same street, the same buildings, the same potential defenders. Each man carries a Micro Tavor rifle specially adapted for urban warfare, plus seven thirty-round magazines and four grenades, along with hollow-ground commando knives honed so sharp the blade can separate the head of a mature male from his body in one slashing arc. Nurit and Alexandra, having changed into uniform, retain their lipstick and eyeliner, so that with their short hair—their wigs ornament the floor of the limousine that blocks one end of the street—they might well be taken for androgynous marchers in Tel Aviv's annual gay-pride parade.

The ambulance hangs back at the other end of the street until the invasion force has taken their designated places and find cover in doorways or lie like corpses facedown in the street, clinging to the asphalt with their fingertips.

The ambulance roof slides back, a .50-caliber machine gun rises from within as steel shields lower behind the vehicle's windshield and windows. A white-uniformed machine gunner in the rear scans four starlight-scope monitors revealing every crevice of the street in ghostly shades of green. On his screens dozens of Hezbollah fighters scramble into the street from buildings on either side.

Using electronic controls adapted from video-game technology, the gunner sweeps one side of the street and then the other: In a kind of mortal ballet, the Hezbollah fighters are blown back by the force of the .50-caliber hollow-points, which on impact flatten to the size of silver dollars. Upon entering the body these tear through muscle and bone to cause massive internal bleeding and fatal damage to vital organs. Only in exceptional cases is there an exit wound.

From a doorway of the café that only hours before was populated by tea-drinking *shesh besh* players a lone survivor of this sweeping fire kneels to fire a rocket-propelled grenade. Perfectly aimed, the RPG hits the ambulance and explodes.

It makes no impression.

He shoots again.

The result is the same.

"God help us," the gunner says aloud in finely enunciated Arab, as though speaking in a lecture hall. "It is a tank."

A bullet strikes the wall just above his head. Reflexively the militiaman swivels in the direction of its source and for a moment a look of deep puzzlement twists his face. The Micro Tavor that fired this bullet is equipped not only with a night-scope but also an eerily efficient integrated silencer.

Col. Gadi, leaning out of the limousine at the other end of the street, fires again. The sound at the source is like a walnut cracking open. At the end of the bullet's trajectory there is only silence.

The street is now secure. Leaving four men to make sure it stays that way, Kobi's group enters the target building, taking the stairs two at a time, while Gadi and his men begin searching the ground floor.

72

Having snaked around to the rear of the building, two naval commandos shoot a grappling hook to the roof three stories above. These are specialists, trained to board fast-moving ships from rubber boats bobbing in the waves by pulling themselves up to a deck as much as one hundred feet above their heads. To naval commandos, successfully making fast a grappling hook from solid ground is hardly a challenge. After securing the other end of the rope to a parked automobile, one begins climbing as the other stands guard. When the first reaches the roof to cover him, the second straps his rifle to his back and ascends so quickly it is as if gravity, in this spot, on this rope, has no dominion.

73

In the single apartment on the ground floor spaghetti is still cooking on a stove in the kitchen, music plays on a radio in a long room used as a barracks, and a cigarette still burns in an ashtray on a card table whose hands have been abandoned in midplay. The ground floor is otherwise empty.

"Commander, over here!"

It is an entrance to the basement, not very well concealed behind a kitchen cupboard that crudely slides away, no booby trap, no security, not so much as a latch. A flight of wooden stairs and there it is, just as they had studied it in the video transmissions: a television studio, oddly larger in reality than on-screen. Of course in the videos the twenty or so Hezbollah militia who stood watching with satisfaction the systematic torture of two young Israelis had not been visible. Now they are equally invisible, having fled rather than confront Jews who are not unarmed, not tied, not undergoing torture. The room is as empty as the ground floor.

A moment later, down a dark, damp corridor, Gadi's force finds a tiny room, its steel door ajar: inside nothing but blood-soaked blankets.

From somewhere above, echoing in the walls, the sound of gunfire.

"Upstairs! On the double!"

74

In an apartment on the third floor, Tawfeek Nur-al-Din burns papers in a fireplace as two bodyguards open a hatch leading to the roof. A folding ladder drops down. The two scramble up. Their only possible escape is over the rooftops. But when the first bodyguard steps onto the flat roof of the building he comes face-to-face with the two naval commandos.

His inert body drops back into the room. With the rooftop blocked, the remaining bodyguard steps on the chest of his dead companion, pushes up the spring-loaded hatch, and bolts it.

"The corridor!"

Trained to respond immediately to his commander's orders, the bodyguard flings open the corridor door and is met by heavy fire from Kobi's unit in the hall. He flies backward, propelled into the apartment by the rifle blasts, dead before his body hits the floor. The door slams shut.

Kobi speaks into his helmet microphone, radio silence no longer necessary. "Skull to Heights, situation." He listens to the buzz of returned communication from the rooftop, then turns to the door. "Hezbollah, this is Israel Defense Forces!" he shouts in Arabic. "Your way is blocked on all sides. You will not get out alive. Your only chance is surrender."

From the other side of the door a voice shouts back: "Israel, this is not Hezbollah, only a poor shopkeeper and his family.

There are small children. Please God, all cursed Hezbollah cowards are gone!" Meanwhile, the speaker continues methodically to burn papers in the fireplace.

Kobi kneels to pull on his gas mask as the unit follows suit. Their eyes are fixed on the door. If they must break in, the room will be flooded instantly with tear gas.

"Whoever you are, surrender before we breach the door and come in firing."

"There are no Hezbollah here. Only family, children. We are innocent Christians. Please leave us in peace."

Outside in the corridor, Kobi is joined by Gadi and his unit.

"We take them out now," Gadi says in an undertone. "No delay."

"I need information, not corpses," Kobi says. It is the classic battlefield confrontation: intelligence requires prisoners so they can be pumped for critical information; operations requires them dead.

"Ten seconds and we're inside." Somehow Gadi's lisp adds to his authority.

Kobi is not about to dispute the order. In close combat, decisions made on the spot may be wrong, but they are not subject to debate. "This is your final warning!" he shouts. "Unlock the door or we will do it for you! You will not survive!" Into his helmet microphone, he whispers, "Skull to Heights, situation." He presses the earpiece to his head. "There's a chimney. He's burning papers."

"On three," Gadi whispers.

"Skull to Heights, on my count of three." A buzz. "One . . . two . . ."

From inside: "Do not shoot! I am opening the door. Do you hear me? I am opening—"

As soon as they hear the tumblers fall in the lock, Gadi kicks in the door, knocking the man inside to the floor as at the same time the two naval commandos rappel through the room's rear windows in a crescendo of exploding glass.

"Do not shoot! I am unarmed! Do not shoot!"

It is all over. Thirty men are now in the room, rifles pointed down at the man on the floor. With a nod toward an interior door, Gadi signals his men to secure the rest of the apartment. He turns to Kobi. "Your prisoner."

In a quick scan of the room, Kobi has already seen the overflowing ashtray on the coffee table, next to it a pack of Liban cigarettes. This is Heavy Smoker. "What is your name, commander?" he says in Arabic with a mixture of charm and reserve. It is as if the intelligence officer and the man on the floor are meeting at a cocktail party at one of the casinos in the hills east of the city, a couple of princelings from any of a dozen Arab countries out for an evening of the kind of alcohol-fueled revelry that is forbidden at home.

The man on the floor looks up with an expression of bemused self-interest. "I trust you will understand about the papers. My superiors would not look kindly upon me if they learned I gave up secrets. I could die by knife in your prisons."

"Name."

"Tawfeek Nur-al-Din, lieutenant colonel, Militia of Hezbollah. Identity number 132613."

"Where are the two Israeli soldiers, colonel? I will not ask this question again."

"Tawfeek Nur-al-Din, lieutenant colonel, Militia of Hezbollah. Identity number 132613." He smiles. "By the rules of the Geneva Convention, I demand to be treated properly as a prisoner of war according to my rank as a uniformed officer."

Kobi steps back. "Your prisoner, Gadi."

"Medic!"

"I am not injured."

"Medic, treat this man."

The medic looks at his commanding officer.

"If you will permit me to stand, I will demonstrate—"

His words are cut off by a muffled gunshot. In the closed room, the efficient silencer causes it to sound like thick fingers snapping. The Hezbollah commander is screaming in agony.

"You have another knee, *habibi*."

"Tawfeek Nur-al-Din," he says through his teeth. "Lieutenant colonel, Militia of Hezbollah. Identity number 132613. What you have done is in contravention of the Geneva Accords regarding treatment of prisoners of war! I am bleeding!"

Gadi looks at his watch. "A bit. Meanwhile, as much as it would give me pleasure to do this limb by limb, we don't have the time." He kneels beside the man and, with his knife, deftly slices through trousers and underwear in one motion. He holds the man's genitals in one hand, the knife in the other. "Colonel . . ."

All color drains from the man's face. "Please, please! Do not do this!" All his bravado is gone. "I know nothing of Israeli soldiers. I am—"

"Madam . . ." Gadi says with a smile.

"Al-Fasi Street!" the prisoner blurts. "The Barbour Quarter!"

Kobi steps forward. "What number?"

"Seventeen. Number seventeen. The first floor!"

"Ground floor or one flight up?"

"No stairs. As you enter."

"How are they guarded?"

"Two men inside. Two outside. Please!"

Gadi rises. "You can keep your testicles, colonel."

"Thank you, thank you so much."

"My pleasure," Gadi says. "Only one thing more."

"Yes, please, anything!"

"The Geneva Convention does not apply to terrorists."

The men holding Lt. Col. Tawfeek Nur-al-Din drop him and move to the side. Gadi does not waste any time. They are not in a position to take prisoners. At this range the 9mm shells are of sufficient velocity to exit the skull and bury themselves in the wooden floor.

75

As the Mercedes limousine moves through the streets followed by the ambulance, Kobi, Gadi, and three others change into the Hezbollah uniforms that had been stored in the limousine's trunk. In the tight confines of the automobile, one of the white ritual fringes tucked under Kobi's combat uniform manages to escape. Six inches descend from his belt at the rear like a horse's tail. No one notices.

76

Number 17 Al-Fasi Street is guarded by two Hezbollah fighters who stand smoking on either side of the double doorway.

"Greetings, my brothers," Gadi hails them in Arabic. "Is it quiet?"

"Quiet like death. Ten minutes earlier there was much gunfire from that direction. Do we know you?"

"Replacements, courtesy of Col. Tawfeek. There was a bit of trouble with the Christians." He draws his finger across his throat. "Now no more Christians, no more trouble."

"We wondered."

Gadi pulls a folded sheet from his pocket. "Col. Tawfeek sends his greetings. New orders."

"When then are we expected to sleep?" the second Hezbollah asks. It is the infantryman's universal complaint.

"Now," Gadi says.

The silenced Micro Tavors of the two commandos by his side make so little sound the militiamen seem to fall of their own will.

In an instant the unit is inside the building, Gadi knocking quietly on the one door on the ground floor. The dark of the hallway is broken by a shaft of light as a peephole slides open.

"Your relief detail is here," Gadi says into it.

"Thanks be to God."

The door opens, revealing a kitchen with a propane cooktop, a small refrigerator trembling on rusted-out, uneven feet, a sink piled high with dishes and a counter cluttered with empty cans of Libni-Cola, and a box of 7.62x39mm ammunition, standard for the two Kalashnikov rifles leaning placidly in the far corner.

"Make yourselves comfortable," the militiaman says at the door. He is a good deal older than the militiamen in the street, maybe fifty, probably chosen for guard duty because he is past his prime—and has more to lose. The Hezbollah leadership prefers its killers young. They are more willing to die. That is why suicide bombers are rarely even twenty-one. The militiaman returns to a small folding table by the shuttered window where he and his partner appear to be near the end of a game of chess, only a few pieces left on the board. An ancient Webley revolver, its bluing rubbed away from years of use, sits on the table between them, probably to be carried when they check on the prisoners—in close quarters a Kalashnikov is impractical. "There is coffee, but the milk has become cheese," he says. "If you will wait one moment while I reduce this amateur to a pulp, I will wash some cups. Housekeeping is not our strength."

"Where are the prisoners?"

The militiaman motions casually to the door opposite with the rook he has just taken. "Secure within." He has eyes only for the chessboard. "Check."

"Keys?"

"Unlocked. Precisely the opposite of my opponent's position." He laughs. "Mate in one move, Jabril."

"Unlocked?" Gadi says. "Is that wise?"

"If they live another hour I will be surprised. Soon enough they will be in hell, together with all Jews and Christians." He spits, then loses interest in theology to return his attention to the chessboard as his opponent shifts his queen. In quick response, as though doing a particularly delicate bit of surgery, he eases a knight into place. "And . . . mate!" Beaming, he turns toward Gadi and Kobi as they move toward the opposite door. What he sees causes him to stop in the middle of his celebratory howl: Kobi's ritual fringes trailing behind him.

"Jews! Jews are here!" He grabs the revolver from the table and fires. A revolver is dependable that way. With no safety it is the ultimate weapon of instinct.

Before the other chess player can rise both militiamen are cut down. One falls to the floor, the other onto the chessboard, the pieces flying.

Gadi speaks into his helmet-microphone. "Medical team on the double. Medical team—now!"

While one of the commandos applies a pressure bandage to stanch the bleeding from Kobi's back, Gadi and the others rush through the door into the second room. Salim is squatting in a corner, talking to himself about a horse. On the stained cement floor Ari lies unconscious.

77

In Caesarea, Dahlia climbs out of the pool, wrapping one towel around her hair and another around her naked body. She lights a cigarette and stands smoking for a while. Then she enters the living room and leans down to her husband. "Dudik, Dudik."

He doesn't stir.

"Oh, shit, Dudik. Don't leave me alone," she says. "I'm so scared."

Dudik sleeps on.

78

As the ambulance careens through the dark streets of Beirut Dr. Itzik works feverishly to stabilize his patient. Ari is hooked up to a respirator and an IV line but remains unconscious. Another member of the medical team injects Salim. Though strapped down, he thrashes about as though electrically shocked, his body a mass of protoplasm uncontrolled by any higher function, his mouth askew, mumbling, then shouting, then whispering in a mixture of Arabic and Hebrew. In less than a minute the sedative takes over, his body relaxes, drool dropping from the side of his mouth in a long line of spittle that slowly stretches down to the ambulance floor. The team is finally able to get an IV line into him.

A medic checks the stretcher suspended above the Bedouin. The monitors mounted on the ambulance wall are steady but offer no other reason for optimism: heart rate sluggish, blood pressure high, temperature slowly rising. The patient's bleeding is stanched, but there is no telling what is going on inside Kobi's inert body. The bullet entered his back just below the line of his diaphragm. He is unconscious.

"He wants to live. You can see that."

"Who doesn't?" the other medic says. "But he doesn't have all the time in the world."

"I hear he became a cop. Odd for a religious."

"Yeah," the second medic says. He turns to Dr. Itzik. "No change."

Behind the two stretchers, the machine gunner stares determinedly at his screens as the ambulance approaches the roadblock with the burning fifty-gallon oil drums. In front of him he sees the men in the limousine firing from both sides. The machine gunner opens up as well, aiming above the limo and then swiveling the gun to cover the UN bus following behind.

On another route, three of the four original motorcyclists, still in uniform as Police du Liban, speed through another roadblock. It is set up to stop cars. The motorcyclists zigzag through so quickly the militiamen are unable to react.

79

In Caesarea, Dahlia makes coffee. She thinks: *What a cliché I've become. Modern Israeli working mother with luxury kitchen, the best appliances, two sinks, a dishwasher so silent the red lights on its electronic control panel are the only indication it is on. All this,* she thinks, *and I can't remember when last I cooked a meal. Dudik stopped coming home for supper years ago, the boys live on pita and hummus, and all I do in here is make coffee and eat cold fruit out of an otherwise empty refrigerator.* The milk has gone sour. She finds a tub of vanilla ice cream in the freezer and adds two tablespoons to her coffee, then puts the mug in the microwave to reheat. *Would it have been different if I'd stayed home, created a welcoming nest for my husband and sons? Not much,* she tells herself. *Dudik still would not be coming home for supper, the boys still would have little patience for scheduled meals.* It was the way she herself had grown up after her father died. Never much of a housewife, with no husband Erika had ceased preparing so much as a sandwich for her daughter. Dahlia remembers telling her mother, "I can't eat politics." In response Erika offered only the derisive laugh that was to harden into her very face. "They're destroying our country, our leaders, and all you can think of is bread and jam." She had looked hard at her mother, a daughter torn between voiced anger and mute despair. "I'll settle for bread," she had said. All through high school she took her daily suste-

nance in the school cafeteria. Only when she visited Zeinab did she have the luxury of an entire meal, seated with her aunt's family, her "cousins"—seven of them, then six, then five, as over time they were married off and left home—and Mohammed, now Edward, who pretended she did not exist. To Dahlia it was as if she were in her proper place and he the guest. Perhaps he felt it, too.

She is aware of Dudik's presence before he speaks.

"Is there coffee for me, or does that stop after the divorce filing?"

"There's no milk. I can—"

"Black, then. Have you slept at all?"

"A bit."

"Did you ever think," he asks, taking down a mug from the neat stack in the cabinet above the silent dishwasher, "that if we had done something right . . ."

"Right?"

"Different. That this would not have happened? That everything would be . . . different? You and me, the boys. Ari . . ."

"You're just torturing yourself."

He adds sugar to the mug, three spoons. He never takes it sweet. "Who better to do the job?"

They are both looking at the phone when, so abruptly they jump, it rings.

80

At 3:47 A.M. the rescue force is southbound over the Mediterranean, all personnel and the original vehicles securely repacked into the two Yasurs. Flying in formation with these is a late addition, another Yasur that is a fully staffed flying hospital carrying three patients. The six Super Apaches escort the Yasurs along the shoreline like anxious parents watching a baby's first steps. Dr. Itzik and the battle medics who tended to the wounded in the ambulance are with their comrades in the invasion team. They have been replaced by a complete trauma unit in the flying hospital: four physicians—three of them surgeons—and six nurses. They move efficiently and purposively among the patients. Working with a portable CAT scan, within minutes the team has prioritized treatment. These are specialists.

Unless ordered otherwise, the helicopter is en route to Hadassah Medical Center in Jerusalem.

The physician in charge, Major (Res.) Raz, summarizes the situation to Medical Corps HQ on the ground at Tel HaShomer in central Israel. "Medevac Aleph to Medcorps Skull. Three matchsticks. Priority one, Barr, Ariel, 35796518. Ruptured spleen, unilateral pneumothorax due to splintering of ribs five, six, and seven, plus sinister costochondral separation. Zero kidney function as result of bilateral blunt trauma. Apparent devascularization of renal pedicule. This is a priority one. Second

THE LIE

patient, Ibn-Aziz, Salim, 29793651. Multiple blunt trauma with cranial damage, including fissuring. Encephalopathy. Myoclosis. Delirium. Extensive epidural hematoma. Circumferential nystagmus. Patient is sedated. Over."

From the loudspeaker: "Medcorps Skull to Medevac Aleph. Razi, you said three. Over."

"I beg your pardon. Three? Over."

"You said three matchsticks. Over."

Within the noisy helicopter a thick silence descends like a heavy damp quilt. Suddenly, no one is making eye contact, each of the personnel aboard finding something to stare at other than one another.

"Medevac Aleph to Medcorps Skull. I assumed you knew. Over."

One of the nurses pulls a sheet over Kobi's face.

81

In Dudik's BMW they make Jerusalem in fifty-two minutes, stopping only once when a highway patrol car pulls them over near Hadera. The traffic cop has clocked them at 260 kilometers per hour on a stretch of highway marked 110. Dahlia shows her ID.

Immediately they are off, Dudik barely able to keep up behind the flashing lights and the penetrating wa-wa of the siren that flows over them in waves, like a wake.

Just before dawn they reach Hadassah. The head duty nurse escorts them from the lobby to a side elevator marked EMERGENCY USE ONLY. As it rises the nurse says, "Are you all family members?"

Dahlia feels suddenly faint. She clutches Uri for support against the news. Somehow she never thought it would come like this, in an elevator, from a nurse as expressionless as steel plate.

"Mother, father, son," Dudik says.

"Is Ari adopted?"

"What?"

"Mr. Barr, there is the matter of blood type."

"Just say how he is."

"Mrs. Barr, I am not in a position."

"Put yourself in a position."

THE LIE

The doors open. Opposite them is a sign: HEMATOLOGY.

"For the moment he's all right. Considering."

"Considering?" Dahlia says.

"Dr. Samuels will speak with you. Officially, it's not my place."

Dahlia presses. "Unofficially, then. It's our son."

"Unofficially, your son has suffered a good deal of internal damage. They're working on him now."

"I want to see this Samuels."

"In time," the nurse says, her face softening. "He is in the operating room. One of the best, London-trained. Look, we have to type your blood. It won't take long."

"I want to see my son."

"Please, Mrs. Barr. Ten minutes. That's all. It's for the boy, for his good. That's all I know."

"I don't believe you," Dahlia says even as she is eased into a chair with a single padded armrest. A young phlebotomist, pretty and black, with a peculiar accent—probably a nursing student from one of the African countries still maintaining diplomatic relations with Israel—begins to draw Dahlia's blood. "What is this for?"

For answer, Dudik is given her place in the chair.

"Now the young man," the head duty nurse says.

"You know this is outrageous," Dudik says. "Hadassah is opening itself up to a lawsuit for the ages. And I will name you as well—personally. We want to see our son!"

Dahlia looks at him. Her husband's mind works instinctively, she thinks. *He is the real lawyer in the family. I am just an amateur.* She stops in midthought. *Was,* she thinks. *I was that, now I'm something else.* Before her, she sees the face of Mohammed Al-Masri. *Not Edward. Fuck Edward. Edward is just a coat he covers himself with.* She remembers Mohammed as he was, a brilliant student who cultivated good manners to cover his anger. *But we*

205

were all angry then. Angry at having to grow up to die in endless war, to see our fathers and brothers and sons killed, and now—with terror the main weapon of war and the battlefield every school and bus and café—our mothers, sisters, and daughters. At school we were angry at the killing. Mohammed was angry because there was not enough. I should have shot him. There was enough time before Kobi broke down the door. "I want to see my son," she says with such force the African student nearly leaps away as she draws blood from Uri's arm. "I want to see my son!"

82

They let Dahlia in for only a few minutes. Ari has just been wheeled from the operating room: There is danger of sepsis. The two nurses who remain in the room will not let her near. She is compelled to stand ten feet away. Ari's face is white, his eyes closed. He is breathing through a tube attached to his throat. A dozen more tubes seem to be growing from his body like tentacles, some attached to intravenous drips, some to a bank of machines lit by multicolored bulbs and moving graphs that tell a story, but not to Dahlia. The machines hum so calmly, securely, confidently, it is almost as though Ari is an extension of the machines rather than the machines an extension of him.

"My baby, if you can hear me, I want you to know your father and I are working things out." She speaks the words knowing they are lies, every one of them shallow and manipulative, but perhaps encouraging, perhaps that. She cannot know if he hears her. "We're all back together. We're all going to have dinner together every night, the whole family, just like when you and Uri were little. We'll be a family again. Ari?"

Outside, she finds her husband and younger son standing, waiting. They are not permitted in the room. Only one visitor. Not one visitor at a time, just one visitor. *It hardly makes sense,* she thinks. *What damage can family do to the boy that the sadistic enemy has not done already?* But nothing has made sense since she stepped into that taxi in front of Jerusalem District Court and found herself face-to-face with Zalman Arad and ultimately with Mohammed Al-Masri. And with this. And with herself.

83

"I am Dr. Samuels."

The physician is a small man with a tidy British accent veiling carefully enunciated Hebrew, his rug of gray hair cut as short as his beard and the curling gray carpet that seems to be trying desperately to escape his chest through the V-collar of his green scrubs.

Dahlia can see the line etched around his forehead from the elastic of the surgical cap he must just now have removed. His shoes—bright white running shoes, as though he has run an actual marathon and not spent two hours in the operating room—are still sheathed in plastic bags. She waits.

Dr. Samuels seems to be waiting as well. It is a Jewish stand-off, neither party wishing to offend the dignity of the other.

Finally, Dudik speaks. "Doctor, we were told you would be able to . . ."

The doctor seems unsure, as if he is in the wrong conversation. He speaks slowly in his British accent, grown heavier now. Too slowly. "Oh, yes. Of course. Is there something . . . specific . . . you wish . . . to know?"

"I wish to know if my baby will live."

"Ms. . . . ." He searches his mind for the name. To a surgeon, names are of little importance. "Barr, isn't it? I—"

"He's white. Alabaster. I saw him."

"Yes, of course. That's the way most of them, many of them, the way they are." He seems to be choosing his words carefully, as though protective of their meaning, how they fit together, like a frightened witness in a courtroom in a foreign country who is drawing on freshly acquired but limited vocabulary, unsure of the sequence of words as they drop from his tongue, fearful of getting it wrong, perhaps of implicating himself. "Severe loss . . . of blood, failure of certain organs, specific organs, which themselves put strain, further strain, on the heart. He will regain his color. The color comes back. Some never . . . become white. Rose. They stay rose-colored. It doesn't mean . . . much."

"Doctor, we're waiting for you to tell us his condition."

Thank God for Dudik, she thinks. *He can be such a prick, and then such a mensch. Why did I lie to Ari? Even if he couldn't hear, it was wrong to lie. But maybe it wasn't a lie. Maybe it was . . .*

"His condition?" Dudik repeats.

Uri can contain himself no longer. "Doctor, tell us about my brother."

"Your brother, yes."

It is Dahlia who guesses. "Doctor, if you'd rather speak English, please do."

Dr. Samuels lets out a long sigh. The shackles have been removed from his tongue. "Thank God. A month in Israel. A new ascendant. Please tell me what you *do* know." Freed from the demands of Hebrew, he is as much in charge as he must have been in the operating room.

"Ari's been wounded," Dudik says. "Beyond that no one has told us anything."

Dr. Samuels nods. "Let me then get you up to speed. Your son has suffered massive trauma. He has lost his spleen. There is severely reduced liver capacity and absolutely zero kidney function. His right lung is punctured in two places by broken ribs.

THE LIE

The same lung has been partially torn away from the muscles that hold it in place, a minor injury in the scheme of things but likely to be painful because, let us remember, breathing is not an occasional matter." He pauses. "We do have a rather significant complication."

The Barrs simply stand there. There is no use asking what the complication is. The doctor has found his voice.

He drops it an octave, like an amateur actor pursuing verisimilitude. "You are aware your son is a rare blood type?"

The parents look at each other.

"He's never been injured," Dahlia says. "Before this."

"Good job, that," Dr. Samuels says.

"He did have an operation as a child," Dahlia says. "There was no problem."

"Of course were it a simple matter of blood *transfusion,* the whole thing would be rather less complicated. Blood banks keep these rare types on hand for just such an occurrence. It's . . ." He pauses dramatically, a different actorish tick but in the same category: artifice. "It's a matter of renal function. He'll need a kidney. One kidney. He can get by with one. God worked it out that way. Two eyes, two hands, two ears, two kidneys. One of each is sufficient. The trouble in this case . . ."

"Say it."

"Mrs. Barr, the fact is your son will need a replacement kidney from someone with precisely the same blood profile."

"Which is why . . ."

"Indeed, Mr. Barr, which is why we were in such a hurry to ascertain which of you might be the ideal donor."

"I'm ready, doctor."

"Yes, well, Mr. Barr, I'm rather afraid a father's will in some cases is insufficient. Wasn't it Herzl who said 'If you will it, it is no dream'? Unfortunately Herzl was not a physician. Your blood type is not compatible. Your son's body would reject your kidney in a manner most violent. The strain of such a rejection would be enough to finish him. He requires a perfect match."

Dahlia and Uri speak at once, precisely together, and in the same words. "Let it be me."

Dr. Samuels offers a mild, wry smile, at once admiring and discouraged. "Perhaps there is another family member, someone close by?"

"You mean . . ."

"None of you is suitable. This kind of thing, it often skips a generation."

The conversation stops.

"A grandparent?" Dahlia says.

"A grandparent, yes."

"Oh my God."

"Dahlia," Dudik says, "you've got to ask her."

"She wouldn't cross the street to save all of our lives." She turns to the doctor. "What about dialysis? People live without kidneys."

"Madam, your son needs a functioning kidney. Within hours. Unfortunately, not just any kidney will do."

"You've got to try," Dudik tells Dahlia. "We've got to contact her. She can be here in an hour."

"She's not at home. She's here."

"In Jerusalem?"

"It's what she does. This is where she does it."

"Demonstrating?"

"She doesn't play tennis, Dudik."

"But it's six A.M. Who demonstrates at—"

"They've got a tent. They sleep there. Don't you read anything outside the financial pages?"

"I read the entire paper. It's just, it never occurred to me these crazy leftists . . ."

THE LIE

"Leftists, rightists, vegetarians," she says. "It's a virtual summer camp."

"Let's go, then."

"No."

"No?" Dudik says.

"Mom, I can go with you. Maybe she'll see me and—"

"I'll go alone."

"I'll take you, then."

"Dudik, please let me do this my way. You stay with Uri. Uri, take care of your father. Take care of each other."

She draws her phone out of her bag and snaps it open as if cocking a gun. "This is Chief Supt. Dahlia Barr, badge 6402931. I need to be connected with Zeltzer immediately. This is an emergency." A response. "I understand it's six in the morning. That's when emergencies occur." She eases up. "I'll take full responsibility. Barr, Dahlia, chief superintendent, 6402931. Now put me through."

84

In a light rain the Knesset plaza looks like a campsite: tents of all shapes and sizes, some of olive duck and some in the colorful ripstop nylon of naturalists or young backpackers off to see the world after military service. The police car carrying Dahlia and a truck bearing a dozen bleary-eyed Border Police enter the plaza, where the two groups of demonstrators are separated by a line of barbed wire and a wall of portable toilets alternately facing one encampment and the other. It occurs to Dahlia that here, only in the most basic of animal functions, can the two viciously opposed sides be found in peaceful proximity.

"Bloody hell," the constable driving her says. "How do we tell them apart?"

"You see the two flagpoles?"

"Yeah."

"One of them is at half-mast."

"That's the one?"

"That's the one."

"Who died?"

"According to them," she says, "democracy, justice, socialism—take your pick. Park here."

Even as Dahlia sets foot on the flagstone pavement, the officer commanding the Border Police unit has his men out of the truck and lined up. They are in full riot gear.

He salutes her. "Commander?"

"We will need to do this tent by tent."

The officer does not even bother to acknowledge the order. "You four with the chief super. The rest stand by."

The four follow Dahlia in single file like heavily armed goslings.

She stops at the first tent: three men and an incredibly pacific dog, a brown Labrador, which wags its tail and then burrows down next to its master.

In the second tent, a bright red and yellow affair with a multitude of zippers and flaps, a young couple in the same sleeping bag are shocked awake. They are so tightly entwined they can hardly sit up.

"Where is Erika Fine?"

The two look at her and the Border Policemen behind her with an unpleasant mixture of moral rectitude and bravado. "We speak no Hebrew," the boy says in thick English. He is perhaps nineteen. German, probably, or Austrian. Maybe Swiss.

"Where is Erika Fine?" Dahlia repeats in English. "Which tent?"

"If we knew, we wouldn't tell the police," the boy says. "In every fascist country, it is the same."

"Have a nice day," Dahlia says.

In the third tent they find her. Predictably Auntie Zeinab is with her. Between their air mattresses are an empty red plastic milk crate on which rest a candle, mostly burnt down, and an old-fashioned wind-up alarm clock emitting a loud, metallic tick-tock. In front of the crate is a large aluminum cook pot, the kind used for soup.

"Erika!"

Her mother stirs awake. She takes in the scene as though she has just dreamed it. "So, my daughter is now a full-fledged Gestapo."

"Mother, I need you to come with me."

Nothing, not so much as a blink.

"Mother, I need your help."

"Mother?" Erika's voice drips sarcasm.

"Please. It's important."

Now Zeinab is awake. "What is happening?"

Even in the dim light of the tent, Dahlia sees her auntie has grown old. Her hair, normally covered with a flower-printed cloth, is white, in sharp contrast to Erika's bright red, which is dyed. *It is as red*, Dahlia thinks absurdly, *as her politics.*

"It's all right, auntie. I just need Erika to come with me."

"Police," Zeinab says. "My dear niece, I don't understand."

"What is there to understand? My daughter works for the same police who oppress your people, who have detained your son. Probably even now they have him in their torture cells. I told you about this girl. She is the worst sort of traitor, a traitor to truth. Her entire family is rotten."

"Erika, we can have a political discussion later. I need you to come with me. Now. It's a matter of life and death."

"A matter of life and death. So subtle the threat, Dahlia. Let me tell you something. To remove me from this tent, from this vigil, from being a presence before the Knesset for the truth and for decency, your police goons will have physically to remove me."

Inexplicably, Dahlia thinks this is funny—no, she feels it. For the first time in her life, she has real power over her mother, this bitterly implacable bitch who never showed her so much as an ounce of love. *No fucking wonder I am alone, no fucking wonder I turned Dudik away.* She knows she is being too hard on herself, that Dudik carries his own share of responsibility for their love-less marriage. But at this moment she does not care. It is not hate that she feels boiling up within her, it is vengeance. "Constables, you heard the woman. She demands to be physically removed. I so order it."

THE LIE

Almost before Dahlia finishes speaking Erika rises from her air mattress. With a sullen grace she picks up the aluminum pot and throws it. It lands short, its acrid contents splashing out to cover Dahlia's shoes.

"And cuff her," Dahlia says, leaving the tent.

Outside, the encampment has come to life, several dozen people standing around, mostly young. A girl picks up a rock. Out of the corner of her eye, Dahlia sees the rest of the Border Police unit running up.

The crowd has begun to chant. "Fasc-ist, po-lice. Fasc-ist, po-lice. Fasc-ist, po-lice. Fasc-ist, po—"

A rock flies by Dahlia's head.

As two constables hustle a handcuffed Erika out of the tent past her—her mother has gone limp so as not to cooperate—the Border Police form a defensive line. Another rock flies. Now it is on. The Police unit moves forward, batons flailing.

From inside the tent the two other constables remove Zeinab, likewise handcuffed. She does not go limp, but walks with dignity. As she passes Dahlia, their eyes meet. Dahlia sees it, a tiny smile lighting up the deep furrows of Zeinab's face, a smile of reassurance, a smile of love.

Dahlia is at once comforted and torn with guilt. *Would you love me still, auntie, if you knew what I have done to your son—and what I would have done?*

85

At the hospital Erika remains resolute: She will be the martyr. Only her eyes register confusion: Why a hospital, not a police station? She refuses to walk. Dahlia has her strapped into a wheelchair and rolled upstairs to where Dudik and Uri wait. Dr. Samuels is gone. Zeinab sits on a bench next to Uri, whom she used to watch over as a child. They have long had a special relationship. In the same way that the Arab woman has been a substitute mother for Dahlia, she has been a substitute grandmother for the boys, never seeing them without drawing from the folds of her long dress a biscuit or cellophane-wrapped hard candy.

"Uncuff this woman," Dahlia says.

A policeman cuts the disposable plastic strip that holds Zeinab's hands behind her back.

"If she is tied, I will be tied," she tells Dahlia.

"Give us a minute, auntie. Erika, look at me."

Erika spits in her direction.

"Piss, spit—is there anything else you'd like to spatter me with?"

"Menstrual blood," her mother says. "But I no longer have it. You are a shame to your family. If your father were alive . . ."

"If my father were alive, I would not have to turn to you. Look, Ari has been seriously injured." She does not bother with the circumstances. That would not help. "He needs a kidney or he will die. Mine are no good. Dudik and Uri the same. He needs a kidney. A grandparent's may be suitable. He needs a kidney or he will die."

A smile widens on her mother's face. Her eyes appear to be laughing. "This is why you brought me here?"

"This is why."

"You are manipulating the police power of a fascist state to save the life of your own child?"

"Yes."

"Tell me, then: What happens to those who are not similarly employed by the power structure? I will answer my own question—"

"You always do."

"That child will die. Yours, because of your corrupt relationship with the state, will live. The other will die. There you have it, the very metaphor for fascism."

"Erika, this is not an exercise in dialectical materialism. This is Ari's life."

"What if it were the life of an Arab? Zeinab's child? Would that child have the same chance?"

"Mother—"

"Mother again. When you need me you call me mother."

"You urged me to call you Erika from the time I could speak. But you are my mother, Ari's grandmother."

"Do not evade, Dahlia. This is not a kangaroo court full of lawyers who lie and judges who decide beforehand who is guilty and who is not. If it were an Arab child?"

"Mother, Erika. In this hospital there is a Bedouin boy who was injured in the same . . . incident. He is being treated with the same care. I am told he is on the floor below. Would you like to see him, see his family? There are many problems here between Jew and Arab, but free access to equal medical care is not one of them, and you know it. Not everything may be turned into propaganda. I beg you. We need to test your blood."

"My blood?" Erika laughs. "Foolish girl. My blood is my own."

"Nevertheless, we must know if it is suitable."

"I can't help you."

"Mother," she says, knowing that she is pleading and not caring, "Ari is badly hurt. He needs your help. Only you can offer a chance to save him."

"No."

"Please, mother."

"You want something I cannot give."

"Mother, we have only minutes. Please let these nurses take a sample of your blood. If it is not suitable—"

"You are wasting your time."

"There are no other relatives. You are our only chance. Please, mother."

Erika begins laughing, quietly at first, then more violently until she seems hysterical, her head thrown back. "You don't want my blood. My blood isn't good enough. It never was."

"Mother, for the last time, let us put aside the past."

"The past may never be put aside. It is with us forever. My blood is worthless to you."

"Mother, your own grandson. This is not a matter of politics. It is a matter of precious time."

Erika turns to Zeinab, who has risen, her hand covering her mouth as if to stifle a scream. "My blood she wants. Mine!"

Dahlia has had enough. "Constables, I am giving you direct orders. One of you hold her down. The other restrain her arm. Nurse!"

As the two policemen grab Erika and the pretty African nurse steps forward, Zeinab places her hand on Dahlia's arm. She says nothing at first, but only shakes her head.

"Auntie, it must be done."

THE LIE

"My dear child, release her."

"Auntie, I can't let my son die. Her own grandson!"

Zeinab tightens her hand on Dahlia's arm. "Erika cannot help," she says gently. It is little more than a whisper.

The room grows silent, as though there are only the two of them.

"Auntie, please."

She leans to whisper into Dahlia's ear. "My child, he is not her grandson."

The blood drains from Dahlia's face. She stares into Zeinab's eyes.

Both women are weeping.

Zeinab slowly rolls up her sleeve.

86

Three days later, the funeral of Dep. Comm. IDF Col. (Res.) Kobi Shem-Tov concludes in the military cemetery at Mount Herzl with a detail of three soldiers firing three volleys into the air. As the gunsmoke rises and dissipates in the light breeze, Dahlia walks back to their car on Dudik's arm, Uri trailing behind on the narrow path. Just ahead of them, Sheikh Adnan Ibn-Aziz, his IDF medals pinned to the blue suit jacket he wears over white robes, leads his five grown sons, all in uniform. His youngest, Salim, will sit in near silence in a military rest home for two months until one morning he dresses and, without bothering to check himself out, finds his way back to the desert. In time he will be declared unfit for duty and granted a military pension. He will spend his days grooming the mare, and riding alone.

As is customary, Kobi's family remains behind at the grave. He was, Dahlia has learned, divorced. His wife, remarried, lives abroad. No children, only two wizened parents and a troupe of brothers and sisters, some religious, some not, and their offspring.

Zeltzer leaves next, trailing a contingent from the Israel Police that includes Chief Supt. Zaid Jumblatt and a dozen senior officers.

Some two hundred uniformed IDF personnel—the entire rescue party along with comrades in arms from earlier campaigns—drift off individually, united in dress, separate in sorrow.

It is a delayed funeral. Normally a Jewish burial takes place on the day following death, even the same day, but the prime minister's office has intervened with the rabbinate to put off the interment to make sure the ceremony receives adequate coverage from the foreign press. The raid on Beirut is meant to underscore Israel's determination not to give in to terrorism in any form, and to remind the enemies of the state that the price for holding even one Israeli hostage, whether soldier or civilian, Jew or Arab, will be retribution in kind. In his eulogy, the prime minister hits hard on this.

In one form or another, the Prime Minister's words will make their way onto the front pages of newspapers around the world. However, in the cause of objectivity and fairness and because the international press is convinced that terrorism can be justified so long as it does not occur in their own countries, Israel's side of the story will be balanced by another view. That view will become its own story, one that quickly eclipses the necessity for the raid with a vociferous inquiry into its cost in human life.

87

Only a mile away, in a room in the post-operative unit at Hadassah Medical Center, IDF Lt. Ari Barr, hooked up to an array of tubes and monitors, is barely able to keep his eyes open. Between the painkillers and the fatigue, his attention wanders as he attempts to concentrate on the television screen across from his bed. The woman whose kidney saved his life recuperates on the floor above.

On the screen is a handsome correspondent for CNN whose deep voice displays only a shade of the discreet Southern accent that gives his reporting the ring of amiable truth. "In the aftermath of Israel's lightning raid to free two prisoners of war captured by Hezbollah," he says, "questions are being asked about the severity of the action. Indeed, questions are being asked about its very necessity."

The screen goes to a one-armed man with a scarred face and glasses, one of whose lenses is black. "Why do they need to do these criminal acts?" he asks.

The correspondent's earnest face returns. "I'm here in a secret location in Cyprus with Dr. Fawaz Awad, spokesman for Lebanon's Hezbollah Party. I can't reveal the precise spot. Fearing further Israeli reprisals, Dr. Awad has agreed to this interview on condition CNN not disclose our precise location."

"They come in the night, murdering innocent civilians. Sixty-three people, innocent people, their lives are taken from them. Even children. Five children, my God. And why? Because the Jewish government refuses to negotiate in the same way they refuse always to negotiate. For this reason, sixty-three innocent people are dead."

"Dr. Awad, Jerusalem claims that all the dead were armed Hezbollah fighters."

"Floyd, let me promise you. They say this each time they kill innocent civilians. It is not the first instance. For what? We asked for the release of the Canadian professor Edward Al-Masri, the father of a small child. This fine man was kidnapped by the Mossad, and no one has seen him since that time. This is not human rights. This is evil."

88

The next day Israel's Ministry of Justice announces that Mohammed Al-Masri, known in the West as Edward Al-Masri, is in
police custody on charges of currency smuggling that could
bring a sentence of five years.

At his trial thirty days later, Al-Masri makes no mention of
the cigarette burns on his chest. His defense counsel claims the
funds in question were intended to build a house for Al-Masri's
widowed mother in Baka al-Gharbiya, and that the Israeli government is merely using the smuggling charge in order to
silence a well-regarded Arab critic of what he terms its "racist
policies." He calls for the court to throw out the charges. "Just
as the Jewish State has suppressed the legitimate rights of the
Palestinian people," he tells the panel of three judges and the
international press in attendance, "so, too, does it seek to sup-
press the right of my client to free speech, a right enshrined in
Israeli law."

What he does not say is that a deal has already been agreed
upon between the prosecution and his client: Al-Masri will
not mention the cigarette burns in return for a sentence of six
months, which he will serve not in a prison for common criminals but in a special security wing for Palestinian terrorists.

The deal works for both parties. The prime minister's office
need not defend Israel on charges of torture, at least not now,

THE LIE

during a period of intense negotiation with the United States over weapons purchases; Al-Masri will be permitted to wear the cloak of martyrdom by serving his time with other heroes of the Palestinian cause. And there is this: Among Arabs Al-Masri need not fear violence from Jewish criminals who, he knows, would eat him alive.

But midway into his sentence, a cell-block court of Al-Masri's fellow martyrs, convened in the library of the special security section at Beit Lid Prison, near the coastal city of Netanya, sentences him on a charge of collaborating with the Zionist enemy in giving up details that led to the raid on Beirut and the rescue of two valuable Israeli hostages.

The next morning he is found dead in his cell.

An autopsy concludes the cause of death to be asphyxiation, but that immediately before he was killed he was tortured. Dozens of fresh cigarette burns pock his upper body like bullet holes.

Epilogue

Nearly forty-five years earlier, in the maternity ward of Hillel Yaffe Hospital in the central Israeli city of Hadera, a Jewish mother manages to overcome her pain and rise from her bed. She brings her newborn son to the arms of an Arab mother in the bed adjacent.

Zeinab Al-Masri kisses her own newborn, a daughter, and hands the child to the Jewish woman. The Arab woman brings the infant boy to her breast, where immediately he begins to suckle. "Allah bless you for this, Erika. After seven daughters, my husband would divorce me for bringing another. That is the way with us. Trust me. I will care for your son as my own."

"What's the difference?" the Jewish woman says, holding the infant girl. "A child is a child."